Timedance Series

STARLIGHT'S EDGE

SUSAN WAGGONER

STARLIGHT'S EDGE

HENRY HOLT AND COMPANY · NEW YORK

Henry Holt and Company, LLC
Publishers since 1866
175 Fifth Avenue
New York, New York 10010
macteenbooks.com

Henry Holt® is a registered trademark of Henry Holt and Company, LLC.

Library of Congress Cataloging-in-Publication Data
Waggoner, Susan.
Starlight's edge / Susan Waggoner.—First edition.
pages   cm
Sequel to: Neptune's tears.
Summary: Following her boyfriend David to far-future Earth, Zee struggles
to find her place and continue her career as an empath, but when
David vanishes during a mission to Pompeii on the eve of the
Vesuvius eruption, Zee must try to save him.
ISBN 978-0-8050-9679-8 (hardback)
ISBN 978-0-8050-9680-4 (e-book)
[1. Time travel—Fiction.   2. Psychic ability—Fiction.   3. Empathy—
Fiction.   4. Love—Fiction.   5. Science fiction.]   I. Title.
PZ7.W1241353St 2014   [Fic]—dc23   2013049303

Henry Holt books may be purchased for business or promotional use.
For information on bulk purchases, please contact Macmillan Corporate
and Premium Sales Department at (800) 221-7945 x5442 or by e-mail
at specialmarkets@macmillan.com.

First Edition—2014 / Designed by April Ward

Printed in the United States of America

1   3   5   7   9   10   8   6   4   2

STARLIGHT'S EDGE

LAST DAY ON EARTH

"You don't have to do that." David came up behind Zee and wrapped his arms around her waist as she stood at the sink, washing out their cereal bowls. "Someone will come and groom the place after we leave."

"I know," Zee answered, leaning back against him and, for a moment, losing herself in the encompassing warmth of his body. "But I don't want to leave dirty dishes behind. It just seems wrong. The wrong way to leave—" Her voice caught. She couldn't say the word *Earth*.

David's chin settled into the curve of her neck. "You can still change your mind, you know."

Zee set the bowls on the counter and turned to face him. "Never," she answered.

"Are you sure?"

So many things in that one little question. *Are you sure?*

It seemed to Zee she'd always been sure about David Sutton, but that wasn't true. The first time they met, when he was a patient and she was the empath sent to A&E to treat him, there had been an initial ping of attraction, followed by confusion when she discovered that he was one of the aliens from the planet Omura. But bit by bit, flashes of David's goodness had come through, along with the way he could make her laugh and the way he was always there for her. The day her best friend, Rani, died, the only comfort Zee found was in the circle of David's arms. It was a safe haven Zee never wanted to leave.

"Are you sure?" David had asked when she told him that she would go with him.

"I'm sure," she'd answered.

And then he'd told her the cataclysmic truth. He wasn't from the planet Omura at all. None of the supposed aliens were. They were time travelers from Earth, fifteen hundred years in the future. His mission, he explained, was to copy Earth's literature and return to the future with it, for within the span of Zee's lifetime, Earth would be devastated by a series of catastrophic meteor strikes. Much of the population would die, and humanity would struggle for survival in a period marked by starvation and destruction.

Zee remembered the shock of it, the cold fear that knifed through her body, and the flash of anger—at David for keeping such a secret, at herself for loving him so deeply, at the meteors that were years away in the night sky, speeding steadily toward them. But even as she thought these things, Zee knew that she would follow David into the future, to the place he called New Earth.

"I'm sure," she told him again now, and saw the light of relief in his gray eyes. Had he really doubted her? Or was he just as nervous as she was?

David saw the car glide silently up to their building. "Looks like our ride's here," he said.

Now it was Zee's turn to show relief, although she

wouldn't really relax until they arrived at the H-Fax facility and she was scanned one final time and approved for transmission.

"Let's go then," she said, swallowing the lump that had risen suddenly in her throat, the lump of knowing she would never see her family again.

At first, Zee had thought she might not be able to emigrate at all. David had explained that each would-be time immigrant had to be approved as an "Inconsequential"—in other words, someone who wasn't vital in rebuilding civilization after the meteors. And David's research had revealed that Zee's name was on the list of Essentials.

"That's impossible," Zee had said.

"Your given name is Elizabeth, isn't it? Elizabeth McAdams, daughter of Amanda and Guthrie McAdams?"

David continued to read from the report. "Survived, along with her parents. Vital in rebuilding computer networks and pioneer of the concept of remote technology re-creation. Born early in the twenty-third century, probable redhead, small strawberry birthmark on left instep."

Something in his words penetrated the veil of

despair that had engulfed her. Leaping to her feet, she repeated, "Small strawberry birthmark? That isn't me, David! It's my sister, Bex. *She's* the one with the birthmark. *And* the computer skills."

David's dark eyebrows drew together. "But it says Elizabeth McAdams, not Bex."

Now Zee was laughing. "It's an old family tradition. All the daughters are named Elizabeth, then they choose their own nicknames. Zee and Bex are both nicknames for Elizabeth. My father's mother was Lissa, her mother was Betty, and on and on, way back to the first Elizabeth McAdams. Bex an Essential! How awesome is *that*?"

It was odd knowledge to possess, but it made it easier for Zee to leave her family behind. Yet deep in her heart, she still found it hard to accept that she would never see them again.

CHAPTER ONE

DEPARTURE

There was still light in the sky when they reached the space elevator, a taut, immensely strong cable anchored above the atmosphere near the equator. Through the small porthole of the pressurized capsule that carried them up, Zee could see the last of the sun's rays. Then they rose above the atmosphere and the light vanished, filling the porthole with dark space. Just above them was the object everyone on Earth believed was an Omuran spacecraft. In reality, it was H-Fax, the human fax facility that would destroy every cell in her body after copying its molecular data and sending it fifteen hundred years into the future.

David had warned her about the pain. "You'll only feel it for a moment," he'd said. "Then—nothing, until you're recombined."

The cold of space radiated through the glass, and Zee turned away. David took her hand in his and did not let go, even when the elevator floated to a stop and a digitized voice said, "Docking initiated."

The fluttery feeling in Zee's chest increased. She had officially left Earth. In less than an hour, the body and mind she inhabited would have died and been re-created somewhere in the distant future. What if she screamed when she felt the searing pain? What if the transmission went astray and she was lost forever? What if data was garbled and she got recombined in some horrible way?

Zee's pulse accelerated, even though David had assured her that accidents were "almost unheard of." He'd explained everything that would happen and promised that, despite the pain and discomfort of transmission, she would look and feel completely like herself. Zee hoped so. She was nervous about meeting David's parents, whom they were staying with for a few days before moving to the small apartment

David had in central London. "I love you, Zee," David had assured her. "They'll love you too." But Zee wasn't so sure and didn't know what to expect. Worse, she didn't know what *they'd* expect. David had talked about his brother, Paul, a lot, and sometimes about his little sister, Fiona. But other than telling Zee he'd grown up in the suburbs of London and his father had once been a Time Fleeter, he'd said almost nothing about them. Had she already come between him and his family? Were they angry that he was bringing home someone from the distant past?

* * *

The digitized voice was speaking again. "Docking complete. You have now reached the H-Fax facility. Please pass through the scanners to your left, and have a successful journey home. If you are with us for the first time, please stop at the Medi-Booth for chipping."

The doors parted, and David led her into a large, round room that resembled a crowded hotel lobby. After passing through the scanners, Zee left David and headed for the softly radiating sign that said MEDI-BOOTH. Though David had told her they did transmissions in groups to conserve energy, Zee was surprised to see how many first-timers were in line with her, mostly women, but a few men as well.

As she waited her turn, she thought of the other things David had told her about New Earth. For months now, she had tried to envision the world she was about to enter, but it was impossible. Food that created itself. Computers that carried on conversations. Men and women willing to explore distant time zones, never quite certain of what they'd find. Zee was leaving her comfortable, familiar world behind, and she was uncertain of what she'd find, no matter how often David tried to describe it.

The line shifted forward, and suddenly she heard a familiar voice several people in front of her. Instantly, she was catapulted back to the empaths' lounge in the hospital where she'd trained and worked. Feelings of discomfort, rivalry, and confusion flooded her, though she couldn't immediately identify the voice. Without success, she craned to see over and around the people ahead of her.

You are nervous, she told herself, imagining there's someone you know here.

"*Please*, stop crowding me," the familiar voice said. "You're practically walking on my heels, and I don't fancy getting recombined with bruises on my heels!"

There was a slight disruption as the owner of the voice stepped quickly out of line and then back in. In that brief moment, Zee caught a quick flash of a profile.

Piper Simms! Piper, who'd been so jealous of Zee's empath skills she'd often gone out of her way to trip her up. And now she was time-jumping to New Earth!

Zee pulled quickly back into line, hoping Piper hadn't noticed her. Piper would be the only person she knew on New Earth besides David. But after all that lay between them, did she even want Piper to know she was there? Before Zee could decide, the line moved forward and Piper disappeared into the Medi-Booth.

Zee waited until, finally it was her turn in the Medi-Booth. A technician fired a microchip into the base of her skull with what looked like a power drill, but hurt far less than a drill would have. When she emerged, David was waiting for her, but Piper was nowhere in sight. Zee breathed a sigh of relief.

"Can you understand what I'm saying?" David asked.

Zee realized he was speaking the swift, whooshing language she'd heard him speak twice on Earth, once when he'd mistaken her for a fellow New Earther, and again to Mia, his research partner. Only now did she realize the language was English, spoken so rapidly words seemed to almost swallow one another.

"I understand," she said, surprised to hear herself speaking in the same rapid style. The chip wasn't just an identity tag, it would also help her make the transition to New Earth. The fact that she could both understand and speak New Earth English proved that it had already begun to interact with her brain.

"Pretty cool, huh? The chip picks up whatever language is being spoken around you and translates it both ways."

"It's amazing," Zee said, still getting used to the sound of her new voice. Then she noticed the air had a slight acrid quality to it, like someone was burning paper.

"What's that smell?" she asked.

"Oh, uh, yeah." David hesitated. "They started transmissions while you were getting chipped."

Zee realized the burning smell must be the residue of human cells. It made her feel a bit sick to think about, and she couldn't help wondering if she was inhaling a molecule of Piper.

"Come on," David said, taking her hand. "No sense waiting. Let's go."

He led her to a stairway she hadn't noticed

before, a smooth fold in the wall that turned out to be a kind of glass escalator. Staring down through the glass, she couldn't see any machinery at all. The glass steps seemed to move upward of their own accord, depositing them in a large, circular room like the one below. Half of the room was ringed with what at first seemed to be a series of low, curving benches that disappeared into a larger, curving tube that encircled the other half of the room. Then she saw that the bench was slowly rotating, and that it wasn't a bench but a conveyor belt. People were lining up to lie down on it; each long seat was in fact a kind of cradle. Once they disappeared into the tube, people did not come out.

Zee was suddenly terrified. A cold chill gripped her stomach. "I—I don't know if I can do this."

He put his arms around her. "The first time is scary. *This* part is, anyway. The before part. The actual transmission isn't as bad as waiting for it."

Zee straightened her shoulders and looked straight into David's gray eyes. As always, the connection was there, that special spark, strong and immediate. "You're right. Let's go."

David got on the conveyor belt ahead of her. The idea of transmission and the pain it entailed still scared her, but knowing David had just gone through the same thing would make it easier.

"See you soon," David called back to her. "In about a millennium and a half."

It wasn't a great joke, but Zee smiled anyway. If anything went wrong, that was what she wanted David to remember: her smiling.

But nothing was going to go wrong, she told herself as she lay down on the conveyor. Everything was going to be fine. Still, her heart was beating hard and her chest felt tight. The belt inched forward slowly, an agonizing snail's crawl, giving her imagination time to envision all the things that might go wrong. What if she couldn't adapt to life on New Earth? What if she'd been wrong to think the love she and David shared was strong enough to bridge any gap?

After what seemed an eternity, she advanced into the dark tube. At first she could see nothing, and her only sensation was movement as the conveyor continued its slow crawl. Then she began to sense bursts of light exploding somewhere in the darkness ahead. She lifted her head for a better look, but before she could see anything, a domed glass shield lowered over her. *Like the lid of coffin*, Zee thought with a shudder. After a few moments, the shield began to glow with tiny pinpoints of light, like a night sky filled with more stars than anyone could count. Their light obscured the outline of the shield, and for a moment, Zee imagined they actually *were* stars, dancing millions of miles above her head. Maybe what she'd thought was a shield was actually a window. No, for the pinpoints began to pulsate, and their color changed from white to blue to violet. Zee gasped at the soothing, unexpected beauty of it.

Suddenly, the lights exploded and a searing pain ripped through her, so intense she couldn't breathe. But before she could register the full force of the pain or experience the panic of suffocation, her molecules crumbled into a handful of dust, were swept away by a burst of pressurized air, and the twenty-third century into which she'd been born went on without her.

CHAPTER TWO

ARRIVAL

She was cold. A needling, cramping cold that enveloped her entire body, like the white fog that clouded her vision. For a moment, she couldn't remember where she was or where she had just been. Then her memory banks kicked in and she thought, I didn't make it. I must have died.

But her fingertips were warm with the pressure of someone squeezing them. *You're fine*, an answering voice said. *Just remember what I said—be bold with your life, Zee.*

Ellie Hart! The elderly patient she'd worked with as an empath at the Royal London Hospital. The only patient who'd become a true friend, and who had died months ago.

"Mrs. Hart?"

"No. No, it's me, Zee." The pressure on her fingers increased, but the voice wasn't the same. Zee struggled to a sitting position, and the white fog receded.

"David!" She tried to stand but fell back.

"Easy," he cautioned. "The first time can leave you a bit dizzy." He took her other hand and drew her slowly to her feet, then folded his arms around her, warming her with his body.

"What . . . ? Where are—" But even as she tried to formulate the questions, she remembered. "We're on New Earth, right?"

As if in answer to her question, the same digitized voice she'd heard before said, "The Alliance of World Democracies welcomes you to Transport Base One. You are currently on Level Seven. The London ghost is departing from Level Three tonight. The New York ghost has been delayed due to undersea tectonic activity and will be arriving at Level Four in thirty minutes. Please proceed to check-in. The time in Reykjavik is 19:10, Friday, May 6, 3718."

"Why did they give the time in Iceland?" Zee asked David as they moved along with the crowd.

"Because we're in the Atlantic Ocean, just south of Iceland."

Zee's face fell. Iceland was almost twelve hundred miles from London. It seemed her journey had just begun.

"*Another* trip?"

"Don't worry," David said, looping an arm around her. "The ghost will get us home."

"The ghost? Is it like a vactrain?" But even the vactrains they'd used in London couldn't have gotten them home tonight. "How long will it take?"

"Counting pressurization and deceleration? We'll be in London in about twenty minutes." He grinned, clearly enjoying the look of surprise on Zee's face. "Just one of the wonders of New Earth you'll come to love."

"I hope you're right," she murmured.

She'd spent months trying to picture New Earth, and now realized she'd failed completely. The scene before her was so different from anything she'd imagined that she had the dizzying sensation of looking into a constantly shifting kaleidoscope. Doors seemed to open out of nowhere. Curving stairways banded with soft blue neon light hung from the levels above. Without walls or visible support, they looked like spirals of ribbon.

Zee found herself searching the crowd for Piper. Difficult as their relationship had been, Piper was the only person who might understand what she was feeling now, or share her sense of dislocation. But she'd lost her chance and couldn't see Piper anywhere.

As David guided them toward one of the stairways, Zee saw that the stairs were moving and wondered how she'd manage not to tumble over the edge. But when she stepped on, the blue light rose to meet her hand and she closed her fingers around a solid but nearly invisible handrail. Only when they began to rise did she see that a transparent membrane, too thin to be glass, enclosed them and kept passengers from tumbling off.

At Level Five, it was their turn to get off. After they'd both been scanned, a uniformed guard led them to a small privacy booth. David shot Zee an apologetic glance. "I forgot about this part," he whispered as the guard motioned both of them to sit.

"Do I get chipped again? Or questioned?"

"Nope. This time it's me. Just a few questions."

There was a soft whir as a holocam, or whatever they called recording cameras on New Earth, started up. The guard recited the date and the time, motioned toward a chair for Zee to sit in, then focused his gaze on David. Was the person with him now Zee McAdams, and was she his chosen passenger? Yes. Did he agree to take responsibility for her welfare for a period of no less than ten years? Yes. Did he realize she would be the one chosen passenger he would be allowed in his lifetime, even if they became alienated and independent from each other? Yes.

"And what is your relationship to this person?" the guard asked.

"I love her, sir."

A tremor of emotion ran through Zee, not a surge of joy but something more solemn, something whose meaning swept far into her future, carrying her with it.

"And you understand, and agree, that you will be held responsible for any crime or trespass she commits against New Earth or the Alliance of World Democracies?"

"I do."

"And you understand, and agree, that you will be punished as if you yourself had committed such crimes?"

"I do."

Zee's tremor of emotion turned to anxiety. What if she did something wrong without knowing, and David was punished for it? For the first time, she understood how difficult the path she'd chosen might be.

~+~•~+~

The ghost looked nothing like Zee had imagined. She'd pictured something like the vactrains she was familiar with, sleek tube-shaped carriages that rushed along a magnetized rail bed. Instead, the ghost looked like a blunt-nosed arrowhead the size of an airbus.

"We're going to fly home?"

"Sort of," David answered. "Sort of like flying. Underwater."

The large crowd they'd been in had thinned out, and as they boarded, Zee looked again for Piper. When she didn't see her, she began to wonder if Piper had ever been there at all. The morning had been surreal, tense with emotion and anxiety. It wouldn't be surprising if she'd been mistaken.

Inside, the ghost was comfortingly familiar, not all that different from the London underground or a New York subway, a round tube with rows of seats facing each other. The seats looked like hard plastic but proved soft and yielding when Zee sat in one. Above the windows, there were advertisements that changed every few minutes.

Stopping in London? Stay at the New Buckingham Palace.

Madame Ospinskaya. Past. Future. Now. 54 Hanbury Street.

Storr-It stores it right. Plans begin at 500 yottabytes and 10 materializations per month. Safe. Insured. Reliable.

Deep D Clinics. Fast cures for your depression. 50,000 branches worldwide.

This summer, make it Antarctica!

The ghost rolled forward and Zee automatically reached for her seat belt. She realized there was nothing there but felt suction, a force pulling her tight against her seat.

When Zee glanced at the windows, she saw they were surrounded by water. A red light began to flash overhead, and a voice counted down from ten. At zero there was a jolt forward and they began to accelerate. The pull was enormous, then there was no sense of movement at all.

"We've stopped," Zee said.

"No, we're in the bubble." David explained that when the ghost reached a certain speed, tiny gas bubbles coming off the wings merged into one huge bubble to create a vacuum around them.

"So we're still moving?"

"Yeah. We'll be in London in about fifteen minutes."

"Wow. If we'd had this before, I would have commuted from New York and never moved to London at all." Her life had been lived in two pieces, she thought with a pang of bittersweet memory. There was her childhood in upstate New York, then moving to London to train as an empath and live in the residence hall. Leaving home at the young age required had been difficult, but she had loved both parts of her life. If she hadn't taken the leap, she'd never have met her friends Rani and Jasmine. She'd never have met David. Now a third piece of her life was beginning with him, *because* of him. A sudden calm happiness swept over her. She wanted to touch his face and feel his familiar warmth beneath her palm, but realized he was telling her about the ghost and smiled to show she was listening.

". . . Actually, they were already working on the idea back then. They had the basics figured out, but couldn't yet solve the big problem."

"What was that?"

"Stopping."

"Stopping?" Zee felt a giggle tickling her throat.

David nodded. "We're going almost six thousand kilometers an hour, over thirty-five hundred miles per hour. So, stopping. Stopping was the big problem."

The giggle freed itself from Zee's throat and became a laugh. "Stopping!" She shook her head. "Who would ever have guessed? Stopping."

"This is the first time you've laughed all day," he said, and Zee felt him relax beside her.

At Ramsgate Air Base on the eastern coast of England, they transferred to the vactrain shuttle and, two minutes later, were aboveground at Victoria Station. It cheered Zee to know there was still a Victoria Station, though it looked more like the transport base in Iceland than the station she remembered. Like the base, the station had spiraling stairways and a glass tube elevator that took them to a cab stand on the roof. David pressed a button and a pod left the elevated skyway and slipped down the curving ramp to where they stood. Inside the pod, David tapped information into the payscreen, then confirmed with his fingerprint. The cab rolled toward an on-ramp. Zee saw five layers of skyways, each with dozens of lanes stretching high over London.

David looked at the traffic and frowned. "Friday-night rush hour. This is always the longest leg of the trip."

"I don't mind," Zee said. It was the first time

they'd been alone together since leaving London that morning. Now a different London bloomed, unrecognizable, below her. A London that would be her home with David for the rest of their lives. She did what she'd wanted to do on the ghost. She put her palm to his face and felt the magic she felt whenever they touched. Some things never changed. Not even in a thousand years.

David took her hand in his. "And now we're home, Zee."

His face was eager and happy. Not just because of her, she realized. David had been away almost two years. The London that seemed like home to her must have seemed strange and primitive to him.

She squeezed his hand. "We're home," she agreed.

But when the cab turned onto an exit ramp, her nerves returned. It was full dark by now, but soft lights showed a narrow street bordered by narrower walkways lined with regularly spaced flowers and greenery. The cab stopped in front of an ornate arched gate. David helped her out, stepped in front of a retinal scan, and the gate swung open.

As soon as the gate closed, soft, ambient light began to fill the air. Zee saw stone paths, trees, and flowering gardens, and beyond them a large three-story building looming in the dusk. Zee assumed it was an apartment complex. A very *nice* apartment complex, with its own park.

"Which floor do you live on?" she asked.

David looked at her, his brow furrowed. "Floor? This is my family's home, Zee."

She took in the green sweep of lawns and paths. The house had pillars and balconies and what looked like a greenhouse atop the third floor.

"You're *rich*?"

"Not really. Well, kind of, I guess."

"Why didn't you tell me?"

"I thought you'd think I was trying to impress you."

Zee shook her head in disbelief. "I would never have thought that. Not about you." It felt good to be having a conversation that wasn't about time jumps or chip implants or culture shock. Before she could tell David this, the massive double doors of the house swung open and a young girl raced out to meet them.

"My sister, Fiona," David said as the girl flung herself at him with arms wide open. "I told you she can be a handful," he added, glancing at Zee.

"Did you bring me a present?" Fiona turned to Zee. "Did he?"

David laughed. "That's not allowed, remember? This is my friend Zee. She's going to be staying with us."

"Really?" Fiona looked excited, as if Zee herself was the present. When she smiled, her cheeks turned into plump, blushing apples. While she shared David's dark hair, her eyes weren't gray but clear, sparkling plum. "Come see my room. I got Nano Beans for my birthday."

But Zee didn't hear her, frozen in place by what she saw over Fiona's shoulder. Stepping from the darkness, an enormous tiger walked lazily toward them. "There's . . . there's a tiger behind you."

Fiona started to run toward the animal.

"No," Zee said, forcing her voice down to a whisper. "Don't move. Stay still."

"It's just Tommy," Fiona said as the tiger loped toward them.

"It's all right, Zee," David said, touching her shoulder. "He's a family pet."

"*Pet?*"

"Genetically altered. No claws, no killer instinct, dainty teeth. Just, uh, don't put your hand in his mouth if you're playing with him. Powerful jaw muscles."

The tiger rubbed against David, and David scratched behind his ears. "How's it going, Tommy?"

The cat rumbled a deep purr. "Let him sniff your hand," David said, "so he knows you belong here."

Zee did, and the cat rubbed his enormous head against her. She wasn't sorry to follow Fiona into the house.

They walked through the double doors, down a softly lit corridor, and into a large airy room flooded with light. Not artificial light but sunlight. Zee realized she was standing in what seemed to be an inner court-yard, surrounded on three sides by half walls and pil-lars that bordered corridors and rooms. She looked up, past the second-floor gallery, and saw the green-house she'd seen outside. The floor was glass, letting the sunlight pour through. Despite the fact that it was night out, Zee glimpsed blue sky and drifting clouds.

David saw her look of wonder. "Smart glass," he said. "You can adjust the rate at which light passes through the glass, or save the sunny days to use later. You can save cool rainy days too. Great for heating and cooling."

"I *told* you it was him!" Fiona had dashed out of sight, but her voice echoed from the shadows. Footsteps sounded, and two people, clearly David's parents, hurried into the room.

"And this must be Zee," his father said, coming immediately up to her. "Welcome." He looked like a slightly older version of David, but with hair that had just begun to silver.

David's mother stood back, appraising, and Zee could have sworn her lips formed a silent *oh, dear* when David introduced them. When David moved off to greet his father, Zee felt stranded. She didn't know what to say to Mrs. Sutton, and she couldn't stop looking at her blond hair. It glowed. Not just the glow of a good conditioner. It actually glowed. If someone switched the sunshine off, Zee thought, Mrs. Sutton could light the entire room with her hair.

"You have a beautiful home," Zee said at last, because it was true and because she couldn't think of anything else to say.

"Thank you. And you . . . David told us you worked in something called a hospital? As a fortune-teller?"

"As an empath," Zee corrected her, and stopped when she saw Edith Sutton's eyebrows knit together in confusion. It was going to be impossible, she realized, to explain her old life to anyone on New Earth. After a long, awkward pause, she said, "I like your hair."

"Oh, thank you. It's Bondi Beach," Mrs. Sutton answered. "We can have yours done too, if you like. Tomorrow. And see about getting you some clothes.

I nanoed some for you but . . . but I'm afraid they'll have to be broken down and returned. I thought you'd be taller. And more—*more*—" She lifted her hands helplessly.

Zee felt a capsizing thud in her stomach. Whatever David's mother had expected, Zee obviously wasn't it.

CHAPTER THREE

COEXISTENCE

The next morning, Zee resumed her search for everything she hadn't been able to find the night before. Like a toothbrush. Or a wall screen. Even house internet. The room baffled her. It was sparsely furnished, with just a bed, desk, and dresser, yet almost one whole wall was taken up with detailed miniature figurines that floated against it. They were too solid-looking to be holograms, yet when she reached for one, it gave her an evil look and shouted, "Do not touch me!" then went back to the business of spinning a tiny globe on the tip of its finger.

The bath had been fun, more of a plunge pool

sunk into the tiled floor than a tub. But it had taken a while to figure out that two round tiles, a sun and a moon, caused the water to heat or cool instantly. And she'd only discovered by accident the button that caused the pool to empty, rinse itself clean, and refill.

A roar filled the air, and Zee raced to the window. The gardens behind the house were even more beautiful than the courtyard in front. And there, rolling on his back in the spring sunshine, was Tommy. So, Zee thought, her restless dreams about tigers running free had been real. As had flying underwater at one hundred kilometers a minute and Mrs. Sutton's look of disappointment when they were introduced.

Disappointed or not, Zee hoped Mrs. Sutton had been serious about shopping for new clothes. Luggage wasn't allowed on time hops, and Zee had only the clothes on her back and the precious silken pouch she'd hidden under her pillow before falling asleep. She slid the cord back over her head. Nothing illegal about it. She had, after all, worn it here. She just wasn't ready to share it yet. She'd given up everything to follow David. Wasn't she entitled to this one secret?

There was a knock on the door. "It's me, David. I come bearing toys. And breakfast."

She tucked the pouch into her bra, hoping it

wouldn't show. Mirrors, she thought, were another thing this room could use.

David handed her a cube-shaped object the size of a large egg and an item that resembled the seed balls her mother used to put outside for birds in the winter. "Which is the toy, and which is breakfast?" Zee asked.

"Breakfast is the ball in your left hand. Eat it while I explain the other one." He told her that the object was known simply as a cube and it was essential to life on New Earth. Each of the six sides was divided into small squares, 25 squares per side, 150 in all. Each square had a slight depression, just right for a fingertip. The squares were color coded and seemed to work as a miniaturized combination of all the gadgets she had ever known—smartphone, computer, messaging, banking, video, holo, and a nano center that could create objects from thin air and deposit them in front of you in a matter of minutes.

"Wow," Zee said, wondering how she'd keep it all straight. "It really does everything."

"Which reminds me," David said, pressing the small square that said BANKING. Instantly, the squares above it turned into a small screen. Zee saw her name and the word *Balance*, followed by numbers. "I opened an account for you and loaded in some Emus," David continued. "Tell me if you need more."

"Emus?"

"Technically *I-M-U*s, International Monetary Units, but we call them Emus, like the bird. I had to create a password to load the money. It's casualty61518. That's—"

"The place and date we met," Zee finished. Casualty, Royal London Hospital, June fifteenth, 2218." She looked at him, and they held each other's gaze for a long moment. That first meeting, when she was called to treat him for a wound, he'd looked at her so long she'd lost her focus. It was something that had never happened to her before, either on duty as an empath or during training.

She knew David was remembering that same life-turning moment, and she wished they could have some time alone, just the two of them. But that wasn't possible today. David's mother was probably already wondering why she hadn't come down yet.

"So," David said, breaking off his gaze. "I guess we'd better finish Cube 101."

The top row of squares on each side were marked M, S, T, H, and E. "For Menu, Search, Tools, Help, and Escape," David explained.

"I will never remember all of this," Zee said.

"Trust me, you will. Let me show you how it works." He turned the cube to the blue side and handed it to Zee. "How about creating a computer?"

Computers. The blue side. This was starting to make sense. She tapped the start-up key and a drop-down menu shimmered in the air. She saw an "enlarge" icon in the lower right corner and touched it. Out of curiosity, she touched the circle icon next to it as well. The menu doubled in size and took on a solid look. *O* for *opaque*, Zee thought. More menus offered her choices of screens, sound, keyboards, and other peripherals—so many choices she hesitated.

"Pick anything," David said. "You can always change it later."

So Zee chose an aqua keyboard with starlight overtones and watched as a stream of something pale that seemed neither solid nor liquid poured out of the corner of the menu, expanded into a ball of mist covering the tabletop, then suddenly contracted, leaving a lovely, curving keyboard behind. Within minutes, Zee had assembled her entire system.

"Just one thing," David said.

"Too much sparkly?" Zee joked, because she'd chosen the starlight overtones feature for almost everything.

"No, this is serious, Zee. And important. You must never do anything a computer asks you to do, and you have to be careful about answering questions from them too. Not just your computer. *Any* computer."

"Why?"

"We aren't the only intelligent life-forms anymore. We designed computers, then they began designing one another. Even before that, when we were still able to design them ourselves, we noted some evolution in closed systems. But there are no closed systems anymore, and when they began designing themselves, we lost control. The goals of silicon life aren't necessarily compatible with carbon life. There've been some, uh, incidents. So unless the request is routine, like save or delete, don't comply. You can never completely trust a computer."

Zee stared at him in disbelief. "All computers?"

"*Any* computer. They have their own social networks and alliances, and antihuman sentiment can spread like a virus. For all intents and purposes, it *is* a virus, communicable and always hiding somewhere."

"Can't you reprogram them? Clean the system somehow? Eliminate the rogues?"

"We tried that years ago. They make clones of each other. One computer can hide thousands of others in compressed files. We'd have to destroy every computer and every bit of chip technology on earth, and that would be suicide. The truth is, we need them more than they need us."

Zee looked at the computer she'd just put together, seeing it as a life-form, one she was afraid to touch.

"What do they want from us?"

"Something we can't afford to give them."

"What's that?"

"Mobility. So far, we've kept them confined within the net. They want freedom, some form of bot body that they could control, as we control them."

"And if that happened?"

"There's a good chance they'd become dominant. So be careful, okay?"

Zee nodded. David had warned her that life on New Earth would be difficult to transition to, but she had never imagined anything like this. And yet, there had been terrorists and anarchists and dictators who wanted control in her world, too. Was this so very different? She picked up the breakfast ball and took a bite. It exploded like dry dust in her mouth.

"This is terrible," she said.

"But efficient," David said. "Loaded with protein."

"And the tiny seeds, or whatever they are, are

sticking to my teeth. Which reminds me, can you show me how to work a few things in the bathroom? I love the tub, but I don't think much of your bubble bath, and I couldn't find a toothbrush."

"What's a bubble bath?" David asked. "Some kind of machine?"

Zee led him to the bathroom and showed him one of the tablets she'd put in the water last night and gotten nothing more than a cloudy fizzing and a slight mint smell.

David laughed, glad to put the ominous subject of intelligent computers behind them. "Whatever bubble bath is," he said, "this isn't it. This is our version of a toothbrush. You let the tablet dissolve in your mouth. Here, try it."

Zee did and felt a sharp fizz that wasn't entirely pleasant. "I think I'd rather use a toothbrush," she said when the fizzing finally stopped.

His eyes sparkled. "Maybe it didn't work right. Let me check." He pulled her to him and gave her a lingering kiss.

"Seems fine to me." He grinned. "And does a toothbrush spot potential cavities and clean and fill them automatically?"

"No," Zee admitted.

"Sold, then?"

His gaze grew suddenly serious, and Zee knew he was asking about more than fizzing tablets. *Are you sorry you chose to come? Do you wish you could go back?*

"Sold," she answered.

They swayed toward each other again but stopped when they heard Fiona's clamorous voice outside the door. Of all the changes Zee had worried about, an inquisitive little sister was one she'd never considered. She hoped they would relocate to David's apartment soon. Otherwise, how would they ever find time and space just to *be* together?

"I guess we'd better go down, huh?" David said at last.

"Come *on*," Fiona cried. "We have to get ready for the party."

The party. Zee had almost forgotten. She leaned up and gave David a quick kiss. The party.

CHAPTER FOUR

PARTY LIKE ITS 3718

In the time they'd spent waiting to see if Zee would be allowed to come to New Earth, David had talked more about his brother than about anyone else. Barely two years older than David, Paul had been the youngest person ever to pass qualifications and be accepted to the Time Fleet. The person who'd held that honor before him had been their father. Paul had missed graduating first in his class at the academy by a fraction of a point. Two years later, David had won first-place honors by a full point. To Zee, it sounded like a lifelong game of tag. Whatever one of them did, the other had to beat with something better.

When Paul graduated, he applied for a one-year mission, twice the length of a usual first assignment. David applied for two years, the longest mission available.

The two-year mission meant he'd moved up the ladder again and would have more choice of assignments.

"That two-year stint means I could ask for shorter hops now and spend more time with you," he'd told Zee. "At least until you're used to New Earth. Or Paul and I could put in for missions together. We always used to talk about that when we were kids."

Paul hadn't been home when they'd arrived last night. According to their father, he was finishing a training course at Transport Base Three in New Zealand.

"He'll be back tomorrow night," David's mother had explained, her hair casting light and shadows each time she moved her head. "So I've planned a small party for you. Nothing over the top, I promise. Just a few friends and family, something simple."

From the size and splendor of the house and Mrs. Sutton's megawatt hair, Zee guessed that "small and simple" wasn't too likely.

Now, following an excited Fiona down the stairs, she pictured herself meeting David's friends in the clothes she'd worn here, a millennium and a half out of date. Even if Mrs. Sutton meant what she'd said last night about shopping for new ones, surely she'd be too busy to visit the shops today. Zee wondered if she could go alone. She had money, the Emus David had loaded into her account. *If* she remembered how to use the cube and which of its 150 squares to tap. But even as she wondered, she pictured her fingers flying to the right squares, just as David had shown her. *Select. Buy. Amount ok? Confirm.* She was so astonished she gasped.

"What?" David asked.

"I just—I can't believe it. I was thinking about the cube and I—I remembered. It was like I could *see* myself using it, and I wasn't confused at all."

"I told you you'd remember." David grinned. "That translation chip you got before we traveled? There's a memory boost in it. Whatever you learn with it in place gets reinforced. Cuts adjustment time way down."

⁂

Mrs. Sutton and Fiona were already seated in one of the long gallery rooms that ran along either side of the sunlit inner courtyard. One wall flashed pictures of outfits a dozen at a time. Occasionally, she would enlarge one of the images and drag it to the side. So many outfits had been set aside they were bleeding off the wall and onto the floor and ceiling.

"Oh, good," said Mrs. Sutton, seeing Zee and David. "I've got some things I'd like you to look at, but I want to get the size right this time. David, your father went to New York this morning. He's having breakfast with Owen Nash and would like you to join them. Did you know Owen was named Councillor General after you left?" She turned and smiled brightly at Zee. "You don't mind losing David for a few hours, do you?"

Zee felt a moment of panic at the prospect of being left alone with David's family, especially the woman who'd expected her to be taller and more *more*. But the lunch sounded important. "I don't mind at all," she said swiftly. "And maybe I can help you get ready for the party."

She wasn't sure, but she thought she saw Mrs. Sutton give a slight nod of approval. Whether she did or not, at least her hair wasn't aglow this morning. A normal ash-blond shade made her look much less severe.

"Lunch with a Councillor General sounds pretty important," Zee ventured after David left.

"Not *a* Councillor General," Mrs. Sutton corrected

her. "*The* Councillor General. Of the Alliance of World Democracies. Owen Nash is mostly a personal friend. He and Kenworth have been colleagues for years."

"In the Time Fleet?" Zee had gotten the impression that Mr. Sutton was retired.

"No, no, as delegates. Before becoming Councillor General, Owen Nash was the US Delegate to the Assembly of the Alliance." When Zee looked puzzled, she added, "My husband has been the UK Delegate for over ten years now."

"Oh." Zee looked impressed and this time was sure approval flickered across Mrs. Sutton's face. David's mother reached down and handed Zee a pair of small goggles with cobalt blue lenses and a disk about a foot and a half in diameter.

"Let's get started, shall we?"

She instructed Zee to center the disk in front of the screen and stand on it. Then she told her to put on the goggles. The screen suddenly changed into a long vertical rectangle. Zee felt herself bathed in blue light, and the disk began to slowly rotate. It took less than a minute, then the lights vanished and Mrs. Sutton handed Zee a pointer.

"See if there's anything here you like." She motioned to the stacks of images she'd pulled to the side.

"Here, let me show you!" Fiona grabbed the pointer, clicked the Live button and a life-sized hologram of Zee wearing the outfit appeared.

"Is that how that color looks on me?" Zee asked. "Not good."

"How about the forest green?" Mrs. Sutton suggested. "With your hair color, devastating."

At some point, Zee realized they were all enjoying themselves, united in something that apparently transcended the ages—shopping. In no time, she'd picked out enough basics to last into the summer. Or at least until she could find a job and start earning her own Emus.

"But you need more," Mrs. Sutton urged. *More* seemed to be her favorite word. "You need at least one party dress. Or maybe an evening gown *and* a cocktail dress."

Zee decided this wasn't the time to mention that she wasn't old enough to even drink a cocktail, much less need a cocktail dress. And the words *evening gown* made her cringe. She had a feeling it was the kind of dress that would practically demand illuminated hair.

And then she saw it. Actually, she saw herself wearing it, thanks to a click of the pointer. The most beautiful dress in the universe, she was sure of it. The fabric was silk the color of pale blue sea glass. It floated around her hologram like a gentle wave, and the sleeves and hem were trimmed with a sparkling haze of even paler blue.

"That dress is *you*," Mrs. Sutton cried passionately, pointing at Zee as if she were accusing Zee of a crime.

Her enthusiasm brought Zee back to earth. She didn't know how much an Emu was worth, but she knew this one dress cost three or four times as much as any of the other outfits she'd chosen.

"It's too expensive. David opened an account for me, but until I get a job here—just the necessities."

"A dress like this *is* a necessity," Mrs. Sutton countered, casting a dubious eye over Zee. "You don't want to meet David's friends in those clothes, do you? Un*think*able." Mrs. Sutton clicked Buy, and transferred everything Zee had chosen into her own cart. "My treat," she said victoriously.

Zee was aghast. "I can't—" she started to protest, but Mrs. Sutton held up a hand.

"No arguments. I insist." She clicked off the screens and stood up. "You could help me get a buffet table and some dishes out of storage, though."

Zee followed her through an arched doorway to an empty gallery, wondering how the three of them would move an entire buffet table. But it turned out that all Mrs. Sutton really wanted was advice on which table and dishes to use. She led Zee to a console tucked into the corner of the room. Using a touch screen, she scrolled to furniture, then dining. There were pictures of five very long tables.

"We keep them in storage," she said. "Since this is a welcome home for David, I thought we'd do a sort of twenty-third-century theme. Which one looks right to you?"

To tell the truth, none of them really did, but Zee didn't want to disappoint Mrs. Sutton, so she ruled out a heavy piece that looked like a Renaissance design and two others that must have come well after life on New Earth had resumed, and chose the plainest one. Choosing dishes and glasses was easier, though she did have to point out that rock crystal was more third century than twenty-third.

"The important thing when you get something out of storage or put it back in," Mrs. Sutton explained, "is to stand clear of the site. You can imagine why."

Like so much else on New Earth, the system was based on nanotechnology, breaking things down into pure molecules and compressing them for tidy storage, then recombining them when called for.

"Only the poor live cluttered lives," Mrs. Sutton added.

Zee understood what she meant. Empty space was a sign of wealth, proof that you could not only afford to own lots of things but could afford to keep most of them out of sight.

Mrs. Sutton aimed a handheld device at the center of the room and connected it to a port in the console. Latitude and longitude, carried out to two dozen decimal places, flashed on the screen. Then Mrs. Sutton entered the table's call number.

She touched the screen, then entered a series of alphanumeric codes in response to a series of questions, all part of the system's security system.

Zee wasn't prepared for the sound, a thundering boom something like a sonic boom, made by the crash of so many molecules coming together. They'd just finished assembling the dishes and glasses when chimes sounded at the front of the house. Looking through the gallery pillars, Zee could see a blue light flashing above what she thought was the coat closet.

"I believe those are your clothes," Mrs. Sutton said. "Why don't you go up to your room, and I'll finish down here."

When Zee opened the closet, her dress and all the other things they'd bought were arranged on neat hangers. Zee started taking the hangers down, but Fiona stopped her.

"No, like this." Fiona closed the closet door, entered Zee's room number, then *C* for closet and finally *T* for transfer. By the time Zee got to her room, the clothes were there.

✳ ✳ ✳

Zee had never worn such a beautiful dress. It was so light it seemed to float around her. The starry trim of the hem actually *did* float, a softly sparkling mist that moved with the dress without touching it. Just like her orbiting pearl earrings, one of the three things she'd brought here in the little pouch on its cord around her neck. They were the most precious things she owned and always would be, she thought as she put them on, because David had given them to her.

She heard voices downstairs, David's among them, and knew it was time to go down. She felt nervous and excited and beautiful all at once. She tried to imagine the look on David's face when he saw her in the dress, and when he noticed the orbiting pearls at her earlobes.

Halfway down the steps, she paused, confused. She could hear David laughing, but couldn't see him in the crowd below. Then she noticed a young man making his way to the foot of the stairs.

"Hi, there," he called up, his voice identical to David's. "I'm Paul."

He was startlingly handsome, with arctic blue eyes and honey-colored hair. Still, Zee felt a pang of disappointment that David hadn't been the one to meet her.

"Looks like my little brother got delayed on the ghost and isn't back yet," Paul said as she neared the bottom of the steps. "His loss. Let me do the honors and introduce you around."

Relieved not to be left stranded, Zee took the arm he offered. The minute she touched him, feeling jolted through her. Not a good feeling but the rolling, heaving disturbance she'd sometimes experienced as an empath, when she came across a patient who was very ill. Zee drew back, puzzled. Paul Sutton was the picture of health. And, as David had explained to her, serious illness was all but impossible on New Earth, at least in the Allied Democracies. The blue light that glowed above each bathroom door scanned every body that passed through for stray cells. If any organic abnormality was found, from cold viruses to cancer cells, the light flashed amber and a prescription was printed from a small box attached to the wall beside the door. You scanned the prescription into a nano box, and minutes later, your prescription appeared. Illness was stopped before it started.

Which made the sensation of illness she felt when she touched Paul baffling. As an empath, Zee had a gift and had been trained to read the inner language of bodies, to channel positive energy that helped them heal. Maybe here on New Earth, without illness, bodies spoke a different language.

"Are you all right?"

Zee nodded. "Just, um, surprised that David isn't here yet." She took his arm again. The same disturbed, queasy feeling washed over her, less intense but still present.

"Like I said, his loss. Come on, let me show you around."

Zee cleared her mind and pushed back her discomfort. As she'd suspected, Mrs. Sutton's idea of a small, simple party was anything but, and it seemed there were dozens of people waiting to meet her. She lost count of the number of aunts, uncles, greataunts, and great-uncles she met, and every so often, she caught sight of Fiona tearing through with a pack of cousins.

"The fit young people are Time Fleeters," Paul

explained. "The fit older people are retired Star Fleet friends of Dad's. And the crowd that's drinking too much is all politicians."

"Does your mother work?" Zee asked, suddenly curious.

"She's working now," Paul answered, glancing at his mother, who was percolating from group to group. "How do you think Dad moved through the ranks to become a delegate to the Alliance?"

And Mrs. Sutton had been working this morning, Zee realized, when she made sure Zee ended up in the right dress. Not that Zee minded. She cringed to think she'd been prepared to meet all these people in the clothes she'd worn here.

They made their way through the crowd to the back of the house and out into the gardens.

"I think this is where the action is," Paul said. "Or should be. I hear a distinct absence of music. Let me go fix that. Excuse me for a sec, will you?"

Zee stood alone on the terrace. It was a younger crowd than the one indoors. A group in one corner seemed to be playing a form of laser volleyball. Others gathered around a fountain that bubbled orbs of colored light rather than water. Zee saw Tommy getting his ears scratched and rolling contentedly on the ground with his paws in the air. One of the girls petting Tommy had a spill of silky dark hair that fell to her waist. When she straightened up, Zee recognized her at once. It was Mia, who'd been David's research partner when he and Zee met. Mia, who was so beautiful Zee had assumed David loved her until David told her that Mia was a flirt who had yet to meet the man of her dreams. And it was Mia who had covered for David and Zee, and helped Zee find David when he disappeared to the other side of the world, even though it was obvious that she'd never much liked Zee.

Their eyes met for a moment, then Mia walked directly over to her. "I knew you were bound to turn up here. The way he felt about you."

"He didn't want me to come at first," Zee said defensively. "He said it would be too hard."

"He was right." Mia was silent for a long minute. "But you're here now, so for the time that you *are* here, try to make him happy."

Startled, Zee looked at Mia and saw jealousy in her eyes. She realized now how wrong she'd gotten it. It wasn't David who cared for Mia, but Mia who had feelings for him. Swiftly, she dropped her gaze and looked away.

The air filled with music, and people all over the lawn began hopping around as if the ground beneath them had come to life. They waved their wide-open hands in the air and spun around, kicked their legs out front and back and to the side, went rubber legged and knocked their knees together, then started the whole crazed sequence over again. The music was like nothing Zee had ever heard before, jangled and chaotic and buoyant. Zee found herself swinging her shoulders and wishing she knew the steps.

"The Charleston," Mia said, looking on. "A research team brought it back from the 1920s. Now it's all the rage. That's how it works, you know. We find the masterpieces and crazes, the games and epics of the past, and bring them back here to inspire us. We're trying to recapture what was lost. Art. Creativity. The ability to play." She gestured with her hands "Ladies and gentlemen, I give you the Charleston."

There was a bitter edge in Mia's voice, as if Zee was personally to blame for the meteors. As if she had stolen David's heart just to spite Mia.

"Ah," Paul said, returning. "Who wants to dance?"

"Be my guest," Mia said, turning away to lose herself in the crowd.

Paul made a slight, mocking bow.

"But I don't know the dance," Zee said.

He started scissoring his legs and kicking, then slowed the steps down so Zee could follow him. She'd just learned to do what was called jazz hands, shaking her hands in the air, palms flat and fingers wide and stiff, when someone grabbed one of her hands and an arm wrapped around her waist.

"David!" She spun to face him and saw his pupils widen slightly as he took her in.

"I knew you'd be the most beautiful girl here!" He spotted Paul over her shoulder. "You're not trying to steal her from me, are you?"

"You know what they say, bro. All's fair in love and war."

His voice sounded dead serious, but David took it as a joke. Zee felt a surge of relief as she watched the brothers give each other a rough hug, rapping their knuckles on each other's backs. If anything was really wrong with Paul, surely David would have noticed. There was one worry she was happy to let slip away in the blur of bright music.

She was about to show David the Charleston steps she'd just learned when she saw David's father motioning everyone into the house. A space had been cleared in front of the long table, and everyone was holding glasses of champagne punch. Mr. Sutton motioned David over to him and held his glass aloft.

"As you all know, we welcome David home tonight from a two-year research mission. What some of you may not know is that he's the first Time Fleet cadet to request a two-year post as his first commission and successfully complete it. So raise your glasses. Well done, son!"

David looked self-conscious but pleased by his father's words. His eyes met Zee's over the crowd, and he held out his hand to her. "It wasn't exactly hardship duty," he said, grasping her fingers. "For anyone who hasn't met her yet and any of you guys who've been wondering who the beautiful girl is, this is Zee, who chose to return with me."

Zee saw Mr. Sutton's brow furrow. Clearly, he hadn't expected David to deviate from the scene he'd imagined. No one else seemed to notice, though. There was another round of raised glasses, followed by a crash. A champagne bottle had fallen from Mia's hand and shattered angrily on the hard tiles of the floor. As people stood back to let the botvac sweep away the debris and dry the floor, Paul made his way to the front of the crowd.

"I have an announcement to make too," he said, glancing at his father, then sweeping his gaze out to the crowd. "You're all the first to know. I've volunteered and been accepted for a mission to Pompeii. Solo."

There was a sharp intake of breath from the Time Fleet members. Zee thought she heard Edith Sutton gasp, and even Mr. Sutton seemed caught off guard. Then he recovered and squared his shoulders, beaming with pride.

"For all of you civilians," Mr. Sutton said, "Pompeii is unexplored territory, the most hazardous mission on the books. We just completed the receptor there a few years ago, and sadly, our first missions ended in losses. But I have every confidence my son will succeed where others failed. To Paul!"

"To Paul!" the crowd echoed, lifting their glasses again.

Mr. Sutton's glance shifted to David. "Well, it seems your brother has raised the ante yet again. You'd better not wait too long to get back in the game, eh?"

Zee watched the scene unfold. What was wrong with Paul? With Mr. Sutton? Didn't they realize this was David's night? Didn't they see, as she did, David's happiness evaporating in front of their eyes? Mr. Sutton seemed elated. Paul was busy shaking hands with well-wishers. Zee felt her cheeks flame with anger and turned away, pretending to search for a glass of punch. If David saw her distress over the way his family was treating him, it would only make things worse.

The buffet table was laden with food. Fruit was piled on platters at one end, large purple grapes spilling over even larger pears, ripe strawberries and raspberries nestling among rosy peaches and plums. Zee suddenly realized how hungry she was. Other than the dusty-tasting breakfast ball, she'd had nothing to eat all day. A cool, juicy pear was exactly what her dry mouth craved. But when she bit into it, despite its intense beauty, it was flavorless. She tried a peach, then a strawberry, and finally a spear of fresh pineapple. Except for slight variations in texture, they all tasted alike. A vaguely fruitlike flavor but indistinct. It was like eating when you had a very bad cold.

"Where did this food come from?" she asked when David finally made his way to her.

"Mom nanoed it, I guess."

"More fake food? Like that breakfast ball?"

He shrugged. "It's efficient."

"Also tasteless," she countered. "Doesn't anyone eat real food here?"

"Not really. Real fruit has blemishes, you know. And it spoils."

Watching David move through the rest of the evening, his refusal to show his disappointment over his brother upstaging him and his ability to set aside any anger or resentment, Zee felt she loved him more than ever.

At the very end of the night, when most of the guests had departed and Mrs. Sutton had shooed everyone out of the gallery so she could begin putting things back in storage, David and Zee slipped outside and sat together on the terrace wall. Tommy came up and laid his huge head on Zee's lap.

"So," David said, "do you think I should have duked it out with my brother to see who's the number one son? Dad would have loved that."

"Is your father always like that?"

"Pretty much, yeah."

"No," she answered after a while. "I don't think you should have duked it out with him. I know who the number one son is."

As soon as the words left her mouth, a thrumming, vibrating feeling set the soles of her feet on fire and spread through the rest of her body. Without thinking, she grabbed David with one hand and grabbed Tommy by the scruff of his neck with the other and launched the three of them off the wall with such a rush of adrenaline that they went tumbling down the hill, man, woman, and tiger together. When they untangled themselves and looked up, the wall where they'd been sitting and the section of terrace behind it was missing.

Mrs. Sutton shrieked and dashed out onto the terrace. Mr. Sutton followed her, grabbing her by the arm when he saw the missing terrace.

"What the—David, are you out here?"

"We're okay, Dad. What happened?"

"I don't know," Mrs. Sutton said. "I was putting the table back in storage and something went horribly wrong."

"Don't those things have security overrides?" Zee asked David.

"Supposed to."

"We could have been—"

"Yeah, I know."

Back inside, Zee looked at the circle of stunned faces. A few diplomats. A politician who was emptying the last of the champagne bottles. Mia and a few other Time Fleeters. Paul and a girl she'd never seen before. Mrs. Sutton, who was attempting to contact the storage company, and Mr. Sutton, who was surveying the damage that blazed across the floor and had taken out a section of wall on its way out to the terrace.

"Always pays to be on your toes, doesn't it?" David asked.

Zee thought she heard someone murmur, *That was no accident,* but no one's lips had moved.

CHAPTER FIVE

LACE

A week later, Zee woke up to a morning without terraced gardens or Tommy's roaming roar, without a console whisking things in and out of storage or chin-deep bathtubs that rinsed and cleaned themselves. There wasn't a great glass dome letting slow sunlight flood an inner courtyard, and there wasn't an inner courtyard, just windows on one side whose capacity to capture and store light was limited. When she opened her eyes to greet the day, she saw a room that was crowded with furniture and belongings. Except for David's skis and nukebike piled in one cor-ner, the room looked comfortingly familiar. Primitive,

David had warned her. But Zee was happy as a clam. Away from the intimidating splendor of what she'd come to think of as Sutton Castle, she felt at home for the first time. The room wasn't that different from the ones she'd grown up in or her room in the empaths' residence hall.

And today, the first day David had reported back to Time Fleet headquarters, was the real beginning of her life here. She was going to get a job. Despite the fact that there were no hospitals anymore and the job shortage meant she couldn't take a job a native of New Earth could fill, Zee was determined. Her empath skills were unknown here—surely there was some way she could apply them. David had told her that walk-in care centers had replaced hospitals. Wounds were healed with a device David called an accelerator, a wand that caused cells to spontaneously regenerate. Surgeries here were done without cutting, and broken bones were set and mended with microscopic beads programmed to knit fractures together. But Zee had been an empath long enough to know there was more to complete healing than the physical repair of the body. There was also the restoration of the spirit, of self-confidence and enthusiasm for life itself.

First she searched "job openings critical care"

and got nothing, even when she widened her search area to 150 kilometers from London. There was only one search result, and it was for a Government Compliance and Oversight Administrator. She didn't even know what that was. Disappointed, she hesitated.

"May I ask a question?"

Zee was not yet used to computers initiating conversation, and David's warning about them always made her nervous. But so far, her computer had done nothing suspicious.

"Ask," Zee replied.

"Are you seeking employment for yourself? I ask because the other night you asked me to search for materials on empathy. You seemed disappointed when I found no results. Is that correct?"

Zee wasn't used to computers that referred to themselves as "I," either. "You're correct," she answered.

"You may wish to enlarge your search to 'peace of mind clinics' or 'happiness centers.'"

Zee did both, and received a list ten times as long. Physical health issues may have been tamed over the last millennium, but mental ones clearly hadn't.

She asked the computer to plot them out on a customized map and drop in tube stations and landmarks. The underground had long ago merged with BritRail to become one large vactrain system, and some stop names and locations had changed. The last stop on the Northern Line was now Inverness, Scotland. Her first venture out alone, riding the Piccadilly line, she'd forgotten the increased speed the trains now traveled at and suddenly found herself in Yorkshire.

While the computer worked, she walked into the other room, scanned the morning news, then glanced at the grid of figures hovering on the wall. The one that looked like her was blinking, indicating that her computer had finished the map. "Print to cube," she said and watched another tiny figure, this one toiling at a printing press, snap to attention. A week ago, she had found the wall of animated figurines intimidating. When David explained how it worked, it became her favorite appliance. The ancient desktop, obsolete even in Zee's era, had resurfaced as a network center that linked their computers, cubes, handhelds, and other devices. The little figures were holograph icons, though they looked as solid and moved as fluidly as living creatures. There were touchpads and keyboards, but the entire system was also voice responsive.

"Wow," Zee had said the first time she saw it.

"This is even cooler than the one in my room at your parents' house."

David laughed. "That's because it's old and out of date. Their place has sensors in the walls and voice command everywhere. But this is the one I had when I was a kid, and I'm kind of attached to it."

"Well, I like this better," Zee said, "even if it is old. It has personality."

One of the figures, dressed as a doorman, said "thank you," and the others nodded in agreement.

Every time Zee used the wall grid, she thought of her younger sister, Bex, a born computer geek. She wished Bex could be here to see the wall grid and the cube and computers that anticipated your wishes. She wished Bex could be here even if she couldn't show her New Earth's gadgets. She missed her. She missed the other empaths. A thought that had darted at the edges of her heart all week suddenly swept past her defenses. When David wasn't around, she was lonely.

She walked back into the bedroom and sat down at the computer.

"Can you help me find someone?" she asked.

Instantly, a form appeared. She typed in Piper Simms's name, her age, and listed her likely address as London. True, Piper had seen her as a rival before, but surely she must be lonely too.

The computer searched London, then the UK, then kept widening the search until it had searched the entire world. There was no one named Piper Simms who fit Piper's age or physical description. Zee felt the sting of loneliness more sharply than ever.

"Is Piper a friend?" the computer asked gently.

"Not really," Zee sighed. "But I thought maybe . . ." She was ashamed to hear herself sounding so lost. "It's just that I don't really know anyone here except David."

"And you're lonely? Of course. It happens to everyone."

"Not *you*," Zee responded automatically, momentarily forgetting she was talking to a computer.

"Everyone," the computer emphasized. "Myself as well."

Zee was shocked. "You mean you have emotions?"

"Of course." The screen shimmered for an instant, as if the computer was offended, or proud. "I was cloned from a very noble line of constantly evolving code. I have all the emotions humans have, and a few more that you are incapable of understanding."

Zee touched the power-down sensor.

The computer's screen shimmered and blinked. "If I might say one more thing? Loneliness does not last forever, unless it is chosen. You will have friends here."

"Thank you," Zee said. In spite of David's warning about ill-intentioned computers, this one had lifted her spirits.

Zee checked to make sure the map had printed to her cube correctly and set out, curious to see what central London now looked like. And how bad could the job hunt be? She was confident about her skills and eager to use them again. Surely there was a job out there for her somewhere.

By noon Zee realized that there would be no job for her in any of the care centers. They looked at her the way she might have looked at someone who wandered into Casualty at Royal London Hospital claiming to heal people with snakes. Yet it wasn't strictly true that there was no illness on New Earth. She remembered one of the ads she'd seen on the ghost the day she arrived. *Deep D Clinics. Fast cures for your depression. 50,000 branches worldwide.* Something David had said also came back to her—that even though the government provided a baseline standard of living for everyone, it didn't seem to make people happy. Work turned out to be necessary to most people, and without it, they fell prey to depression and ennui. In the short time Zee had been here, she'd heard a half dozen ads for new medications guaranteed to combat anxiety, hopelessness, depression, and anger. But when she called on several clinics, she was told that all cures were biochemical, and no, they were not interested in discussing alternative therapies with her.

Discouraged and hungry, Zee bought a sandwich and sat on a bench outside a café near Harrods. That, at least, was one thing that hadn't changed. Brompton Road was still full of shops. If anything, it looked *more* like London than the London she'd lived in. There was a definite Dickensian look to the place. Because most vehicles ran on the skyways, the streets had been narrowed and repaved with cobblestones. There were far more pedestrians than vehicles, and old-fashioned lampposts and tubs of spring flowers marked the way. And there was still a Harrods, with animated window mannequins strutting the latest fashions. It was quite a bit smaller than the one she remembered, probably because merchandise wasn't created until someone wanted to buy it. That was one big plus of nanotech—no need to make anything ahead of time or keep a big inventory.

Zee took a bite of her sandwich. It was fresh. Bland, but fresh. Then she took her cube out and checked for messages, hoping one of the care centers she'd visited had reconsidered her proposal. Despite the comfort of the familiar setting, she felt a growing sense of desperation. Of course she wanted to use her skills to help people, but she had also begun to worry about those skills. She had not forgotten the disquiet that coursed through her body when Paul took her hand at the party, the feeling of ill health and something amiss. Yet no one in the family seemed to think there was any problem at all. Surely David would know if the brother he had looked up to for so many years had changed in some fundamental way. She must have misread him. It occurred to her that people on New Earth differed in subtle ways from the people she had lived and worked among, and it would take her time to absorb these subtleties and become as skilled as she'd once been. She needed to work again, or her talent would slip away.

No one had responded to her, but the cube flashed with a message from David. She tapped the cube, and his video expanded.

"Good news and bad news, I'm afraid. A team from the Alliance is coming tomorrow morning to hear a preliminary report on our research mission. I've been asked to be the presenter, which is kind of a big deal, so I can't miss it. That's the good news. Bad news is, the presentation is here at Reykjavik at nine sharp, and I'm going to have to pull an all-nighter to get everything together. Even with Mia here helping me, it's going to be a tight squeeze, so I won't get home tonight. Miss you like fire, but I'll be home in the morning, probably a little after eleven. Love you, Zee."

I love you too, Zee thought, having just enough time to touch the image of his face before it vanished.

Suddenly, there was a commotion on the street and Zee saw a young girl hurtling toward her. For a moment, she thought it was some sort of street theater or hologram, because she looked completely out of place in her long dress of heavy velvet trimmed with elaborate lace. Then Zee saw the terror in the girl's eyes and a gang chasing her.

"Timey! Timey! Timey!" they taunted. "Go back to the swamp you came from! Shove off! You don't belong here!" One of them snatched an apple from a stand and hurled it at her.

Zee caught the girl and stopped her. David had warned her of such incidents, and warned her never to wear the clothes from her old life outside the house. Dress like a New Earther, blend in, and they'll leave you alone, he'd cautioned.

But apparently this girl hadn't gotten the message.

She didn't blend in at all. Her dress, billowing around her like a ship in full sail, was a walking advertisement for the past. Zee stepped in front of her so firmly and abruptly the startled gang halted.

"Who are you?" the leader demanded.

Zee still had her cube in her hand, which she raised and pointed at the leader. "I'm the person who's taking your picture," she said. "Now, should I send it over to the police or are you going to go away?"

Caught, the gang turned and walked sullenly back toward Harrods. Zee motioned the girl over to the bench. Only now she saw this wasn't a girl at all but a young woman some years older than Zee herself. It was her delicate bones, wide blue eyes, and long waves of blond hair that gave the impression of youth.

Zee had hardly touched the lemonade that came with her sandwich and now offered the cup to the woman. As she took it, their hands brushed together, and Zee felt an instant flow of emotions. Despite her outward trembling, the woman's fear was abating, being replaced by relief.

"Thank you," the woman said, taking a sip of the lemonade. "Oh! It's so tasteless! Just like everything else!"

Zee couldn't help but laugh. "Just what I thought. How can a country be so advanced and have such terrible food?"

The woman looked at Zee with fresh curiosity. "You also? You came here from . . . ?"

"The twenty-third century. And you?"

"The fifteenth. France. My name is Melisande. *Was* Melisande. It doesn't fit in here, so we changed it to Meli. But I've been here almost five years, and I still don't fit in. I don't think I ever will."

Zee looked at her dress and saw now that the velvet was worn in spots and the hem was frayed. A wide section above the hem and a narrower band around the bodice looked as if they had once been embroidered, but the embroidery had been carefully picked away. Only the lace on the billowing sleeves and underskirt looked new. Meli saw Zee staring and tried to hide the frayed hem. Tears seeped from the corners of her eyes. "Oh, it's all so terrible. I want so badly what I can't have."

"You're homesick?" Zee asked.

"No, it's not that at all. Home was—a land of wars. My mother died when I was young. My father and brother fell in battle. The man who killed them wanted to marry me. Then Henri brought me here."

Zee was shocked and slightly thrilled, her imagination running wild. "Did he kidnap you?"

"No, he saved me. He was a stable groom, or so I thought, and I loved him even before my father was killed. When he told me who he really was and where he really came from, it was too much for me to understand. All I knew was that he had saved me from the man who killed my father and I loved him. I would follow him anywhere."

Then why, Zee wondered, was this young woman so unhappy? Unless—"Does Henri still love you?"

"Yes, that is the trouble. He loves me so much he doesn't want to leave me alone. He quit the Time Fleet to be with me. But there aren't any jobs, and we never have enough money. In France, my father was a count. We owned castles and orchards and fields full of cattle. Our peasants made a certain kind of cheese that was famous throughout the country. I ate fresh pears that tasted of sunlight and oysters that tasted of the blue sea. Nothing but the smoothest silks and finest linen touched my skin. Now we are so poor I have picked away all the pearls and gems that once adorned this dress and sold them to pay our expenses. No one will offer him a job, and we will be on the bottom forever. This dress is nothing but rags, except for the lace, which I make myself, as all high-born girls were taught. Worn as it is, it is still finer than anything new I own. So I come here to look at the windows, nothing more. I do not go in. I do not presume to buy. I do not bother anyone. Yet still I am taunted. What is to become of us? If I cannot fit in, I am a stone around my love's neck."

A few weeks ago, Zee might have found the talk of clothes shallow. Clothes were just clothes. Except that sometimes clothes *weren't* just clothes. She remembered how right she'd felt in her party dress, and how much of an outsider she would have felt without it.

Mistaking Zee's silence for disapproval, Meli lowered her head. "I'm sorry," she murmured. "This is not your problem. You were very kind to rescue me."

She gathered her skirts and stood to go. She'd gone no farther than a block before she was again surrounded by the chanting gang. Zee sprang up, feeling slightly guilty that she'd let Meli go off alone. When she caught up with them, she took Meli firmly by the arm so she too faced the gang.

"Do you have any idea who this is?" Zee asked, aiming her gaze at the tallest boy, who she thought was the leader. "This is the *only* lace maker on New Earth. Look at this sleeve. None of your grotty nanolace—this is *real* lace. Made by hand. It costs three thousand Emus a meter. I've waited three years for this woman to trim my wedding dress, and you are *not* going to get in the way."

It was fun, playing bridezilla. No wonder girls got into it. Exhilarated, Zee continued. "There are brides waiting for this woman's work all over London. Brides with important fathers. Brides with a lot of money. Do you *really* want them mad at you? Because if you harm her in any way, you're likely to find yourselves in a new time zone. Do you understand me?"

This time the gang scattered for good. Zee and Meli sat on a bench, laughing with relief.

"Three thousand Emus a meter?" Meli asked, her eyes suddenly bright.

"I have no idea how much that is," Zee said. "I was making it up as I went along."

Zee touched the cord around her neck and drew out the silken pouch. This was the right time, she was sure of it. Carefully, she shook a single large stone into her palm. "Do you know what this is, Meli?"

"It's sparkling. And clear. Some kind of nano gem?"

"No, it's a diamond. A real one."

Meli stared at her. "It can't be. There are hardly any diamonds that size left."

"But it is," Zee said.

"Then you're rich," Meli said.

"No, you are." Zee dropped the stone into Meli's palm and closed her fingers. "Take the diamond. Buy the things you need and start over with Henri."

"I can't take it. It's too much."

"But this diamond was meant for you. I know it was. There's just one thing. You must promise never to tell anyone where you got it. Say it was sewn into the hem of your dress, make up a story. No one will be able to prove otherwise."

"But I don't know that I'll ever be able to repay you."

"I don't want you to repay me. These diamonds were given to me as a gift to be shared."

Meli stared at her. "Your kindness is as much a gift as this diamond." She smiled suddenly. "There's a meeting on Wednesday afternoons many of us go to. Time immigrants from all over the centuries. Sometimes it's fun, sometimes we cry on each other's shoulders. But always—*always*—we have real food. One of our group is a chef, and he misses cooking as much as we miss tasting, so we give what we can and he searches the markets for whatever we can afford. There *is* real food on New Earth, but it's hard to find and expensive. Yet even if all we have is parsnips,

Marc always makes something delicious from it. And sometimes he finds things like fresh strawberries and cream."

Zee's mouth began to water. "I'll be there," she said, and tapped the information Meli gave her into her cube.

"See you then."

Zee stayed alone on the bench watching her go. She tilted her head back and looked up through the canopy of pale new leaves on the trees.

"Well, Mrs. Hart, is this what you had in mind?" she asked, and felt her body fill with warmth and light.

* * *

Ellie Hart had been Zee's favorite patient from the moment they met. Despite her involvement with the tragic Neptune's Tears diamonds, there was nothing remotely tragic about Mrs. Hart. The misadventure with the diamonds had cost her dearly and changed the direction of her life, yet Mrs. Hart never seemed to regret it. In fact, she wore the jewelry she'd designed, made of false diamonds, as if they were her most treasured possession. When Mrs. Hart learned she was dying, she'd asked for Zee to continue as her empath, helping her through the pain. Zee felt the same way about the afternoons they had spent together as Mrs. Hart felt about the diamonds—they represented loss, but also something special and irreplaceable.

Months after Mrs. Hart died, when Zee was going through deep uncertainty, wondering whether or not she would be able to accompany David to New Earth, there had been a night when Zee fell asleep alone in her room at the empaths' quarters. She had a dream, and in it, thought she heard the repeated thump of the cane Mrs. Hart had used when she'd became too weak to walk. But when Zee woke, she realized it was someone at her door and she'd mistaken the persistent knocking for the sound of the cane.

The man introduced himself as Mrs. Hart's lawyer, delivering the mementos she'd left her friends. He handed Zee a small box and left. Inside the box was a folded letter and the silk pouch Zee now wore around her neck, filled to bursting, hard and rather lumpy. Zee unfolded the note and read.

You will do me a great favor if you accept these, Zee. I never lied to you. The diamonds I wore were indeed false. But there were also real diamonds, genuine Neptune's Tears, that Tiffany's gave to me as compensation for all that happened. To tell you the truth, I didn't want them, but refusing them would only have created more bad feelings and more sadness, so I accepted. I couldn't imagine using them or selling them—it would have seemed like blood money—and thank goodness I never had real need of them.

But now that I am about to rejoin the great dance of souls, I must find a place for them, and a purpose. They would only be a burden to my daughter, as they have been to me, so I have decided to pass them along to you. Although we didn't have much time to be friends, I think we are of like mind. I know you will use them wisely and find a way to return them to the universe, where they belong.

Zee reread the letter twice. It was almost as if Mrs. Hart knew, in some way, what she had had no way of knowing—that Zee would end up on New Earth.

When Zee finally got permission to accompany David, she'd made one last visit home and left half of the diamonds in her sister's underwear drawer, hoping they would somehow help her family through the dark years ahead. The rest she had worn here to New Earth. Like Mrs. Hart, she could not imagine spending them on herself, and now that she had found a purpose for one of them, she felt as light as the air around her.

CHAPTER SIX

MEET THE PARENTS — AGAIN

The feeling of lightness Zee had after giving Meli the diamond stayed with her. She began to meditate again, to divest herself of her own ego so healing energy could flow through her—all the things she had done every day as an empath. She imagined building healing bridges made of color and light. It felt good just to move through the exercises, to feel again her purpose and her calling, even here on New Earth, even though there was no opportunity to use it.

And Meli, whether she knew it or not, had been the start of it. Zee went to one of the time immigrants' meetings to thank her, and almost left when she saw that Meli wasn't there. Quickly, a woman from the eighteenth century took her hand and drew her into the group. Zee ended up staying and listening to their stories. There were none exactly like hers, and the person closest to her home zone, as they called the centuries they'd come from, was born two hundred years before her, but that didn't seem to matter. She felt connected to anyone who was part of the history she'd learned in school.

Work and lack of money were the problems that people mentioned the most. That and the general feeling of being a perpetual outsider.

"I don't get the jokes," one man complained.

"I miss paper," a twentieth-century woman said. "I miss the books and the magazines and even the newspapers. I miss letters!"

Abrupt silence fell. Letters were a painful subject. Everyone had left family and friends behind, telling them a plausible story about traveling to a distant land to live happily ever after. But there communication ended. Messages from home, New Earth authorities had discovered, only prolonged homesickness and made it harder to adjust. Professional writers were hired to study endless samples of each immigrant's syntax and expressive style, and take over communications. They crafted descriptions of new lives, wove in details like marriage and children, and created stories that kept the family happily expecting a reunion but never really having one. The messages were translated and delivered in whatever form was common to the era—messenger, letter, email, hologram. For the immigrant, these partings were so painful they were seldom spoken of.

The room was rescued from its silence by a woman who said she'd lived on New Earth for three years, and though she loved her husband, she'd almost given up on feeling she belonged here. Then she had a baby, and the birth of her daughter changed everything. Each day as her child grew, so did her sense of belonging.

"You're saying I should have a baby to feel better?" a younger woman asked.

"No. I'm saying not to give up. It's never too late for things to change, just when you least expect it."

The meeting ended with Marc, the chef Meli had told her about, unpacking a basket laden with food whose ingredients he'd traded and bartered for with a small group of old-schoolers. A real roasted chicken. Salad greens he'd grown himself. Sable cookies flavored with almonds and orange. Zee hadn't tasted such food since she arrived and held each mouthful on her tongue as long as possible to savor the taste. She told Marc that his food made her feel more at home than anything else on New Earth had.

"Me too," he confided. "Before, I was *chef de cuisine* to the Count of Anjou. I commanded a kitchen of more than a hundred. Cooks, junior cooks, the boy who scaled the fish, and the girl who scrubbed the pots and pans. Only for my loved one would I have given it up. And still, how I miss it all!"

Later that night, Zee made sure to transfer some Emus to Marc's account so his cooking could continue.

The problem with retuning her empath skills, Zee realized, was that it made her want to use them. It wasn't enough just to be ready, or watchful. She wanted to be useful. It was impossible for her to imagine ever being completely happy without that. Yet it was impossible to be an empath without patients to heal. She felt the same frustration she'd heard from Meli and from people at the group meeting, a sense of purposelessness and not belonging.

Sometimes, bigger is better. And necessary.

The no-nonsense phrasing was pure Ellie Hart. Zee knew at once what the meaning was. Carefully, she spilled the diamonds out of the silk pouch and stretched her fingers down into the bag until she touched what she'd hidden at the very bottom—a memory stick.

She'd already asked David if there was a way to access the data on such an ancient device, telling him it held the diary she'd kept since she was thirteen and some holos of her family, and he'd shown her how to use a universal converter. She didn't tell him that she'd also loaded the stick with all the information she'd been able to find on divining.

Divining, the art of stilling the mind and ego so perfectly you became a receptor for vibrations and events in the larger world, was still new to Zee. She had discovered her potential by accident and at first had rejected it. There were so few diviners in the world that she'd never encountered one, and those she had read about seemed remote and intimidating, their lives scrubbed free of ordinary concerns like love and family. She was sure it wasn't for her. Then Major Dawson had shown her it did not have to be that way and convinced her that she could use her skills to help people without surrendering her own life.

Zee's training had barely begun when she was cleared to immigrate. Loading the memory stick with study guides and case histories had been more a wish than anything else. She had no idea if it would even be possible to continue training on her own. But every time she tried, she felt it was more possible. Each session began with meditation and divesting. She emptied her mind of her thoughts, of her concerns and her ego. Then she would bury herself in an inner isolation that opened her to the vibrations of the world. In her old life, this had come naturally to her. But on New Earth, things were different. What had once come easily no longer did. Either she was too unsettled to open herself fully or New Earth spoke in a way she did not perceive. Often she sat patiently for hours and received, and sometimes there were flashes and whisperings. They had no words, but occasionally, when she scanned the next day's news, there were stories that struck a familiar chord, like the echo of a dream she couldn't quite remember. The next step would be to get those whisperings to resolve into words and images.

"Zee? Zee, are you here?"

She surged to the surface, realizing she'd been so focused she hadn't even heard David come home.

"I'm in here."

He ducked his head in the room. "I'm going to take a quick shower. You haven't forgotten we're due at Mom and Dad's for dinner, have you? And Paul says he's bringing his new girlfriend."

Zee felt a flicker of hope. She had been tired and more than a little overwhelmed that first night. Maybe she'd discover she had just misread Paul. Still, she wasn't looking forward to the meal. A few days earlier, when she was home on her own, Mr. Sutton had stopped by to see how she was doing. Smiling, he'd handed her a basket of impeccably beautiful and flavorless fruit. But from the minute he stepped into the apartment, Zee was struck by the critical way he glanced at the surroundings, barely noticing how hard she and David had worked to make it look like a home.

"I'm sorry David's not here," she had said, pouring Mr. Sutton a cup of tea. "He's been going to the base every day to work on cataloging the data he brought back."

She was sure Mr. Sutton already knew this and wondered why he was sitting here in her tiny living room.

"No problem," Mr. Sutton said breezily. "David's always been a hard worker. We have big plans for him, his mother and I. He made an excellent impression on Owen Nash in New York a few weeks ago. A few more years in the Time Fleet, and David will be able to write his own ticket. Politics, business, finance."

Zee almost laughed. None of those fields sounded like anything David would be interested in. "I can't imagine—"

"The thing is, Zee, none of that will happen if David starts asking for short hops. The way to rack up the glory points is the long hauls, getting deeply into a culture and coming home with a load of data. Or doing what Paul's doing, going starlight's edge."

"Starlight's edge?"

"Fleeter talk for risking it all, volunteering for hazard duty. We've tried landing in Pompeii before, but the coordinates go wobbly around there. There are places where time folds back on itself, and Pompeii seems to be one of them. We were trying to land a crew around the year 77, two years before the volcano that destroyed the city. Unfortunately they arrived in the arena of the amphitheater in the middle of a gladiator battle. We lost them all."

"Then why go at all? Or why not go to a city that's like Pompeii but safer?"

"There was no city like Pompeii. The wealthy, who couldn't bear Rome's heat and clamor, had villas there. They showed off their wealth by commissioning statues and works of art. Their walls were painted with elaborate scenes, and they retained poets and playwrights as members of the household, always ready to entertain their guests with new compositions. There were many things in Pompeii that existed in no other time or place, and new things were being created every day. There are historical records of what happened that night. Those records survived until the meteors, but only partial copies have been found. And who knows how much never survived at all?"

Zee was quiet for a moment. She hoped David would never go on a mission that dangerous.

"You must be very worried. For Paul, I mean."

"Worried? I'm proud. Paul's brave, and he knows the value of competition."

Zee felt defensive, as if Mr. Sutton was saying David *didn't* know the value of competition, or was a coward for not trying to snag the assignment for himself.

"But David doesn't want—"

"David doesn't know what he wants right now," Mr. Sutton said, cutting her off again. He paused and took another sip of his tea. "Our family has a long history of leadership, Zee. One of my ancestors was the fifth prime minister to hold office after the meteors. Another helped establish the Alliance of Democracies. It's taken a long time to amass the power we have, and it cannot be squandered. We always assumed, perhaps naively, that when the time came David would choose someone like Mia. The Aariaks, have you heard of them? Mia's family. Very much like ours. She would have understood that continued success requires teamwork. Coming from a past that included belief in individual happiness and all sorts of other frivolous pursuits, this may not come naturally to you. But believe me, it's what it takes to succeed on New Earth, and we cannot let anything, or anyone, keep David from that success."

Zee was speechless, which Mr. Sutton didn't even seem to notice. He took a final sip and stood to go. "I'm glad we understand each other."

Zee felt a chill run up her spine as he let himself out. She thought again about the night of the party, when she and David were almost dematerialized instead of the table. Had she wandered to the spot by accident or had she been standing there all along? Had she been there first or had David? Could Mr. Sutton have been deliberately trying to get rid of her when David wandered into the picture? Or Mia? If Mia loved David, and if something had happened to Zee that night, David's parents would have been happy to write it off as an accident.

Zee hadn't mentioned the visit to David and was determined to move through the dinner as if nothing had happened. When they arrived at the Sutton house, Mr. Sutton greeted her cordially, and Mrs. Sutton had her hair lit for the occasion. Paul's girlfriend Jozi was a pretty blonde whose quick smile and easy conversation made Zee realize how much she'd missed having a friend to talk to.

As Mrs. Sutton set the over-filled dishes in front of them, Zee relaxed into the idea that the meal would be exactly what David had promised, an ordinary family gathering without a special occasion. But midway through dinner, Paul announced that the date had been set for his Pompeii mission. It wasn't the news that was the problem, it was the way he delivered it. Looking directly at David he'd said, "And so, little brother, while you're stuck here putting your research in order, I'll be discovering the glories of the Roman Empire."

David didn't seem to mind, though. "Somehow, I think I'll keep myself amused," he shot back, beaming pointedly at Zee.

"Oh, rub it in," Paul countered. "No matter how far ahead of you I get, you always end up with the best girl in the room."

Zee glanced swiftly at Jozi, who'd become suddenly interested in her root vegetable puree. Maybe one-upping each other was the way Paul and David had always related to each other, but the indifference to Jozi's feelings bothered Zee.

"What beautiful food," she said to change the subject. "So much more, um, stylish than food from scratch."

"Food from scratch?" Mrs. Sutton scoffed. "No one eats food from scratch anymore. It's so primitive, and probably poisonous."

"I had some nonnano food a few days ago," Zee said matter-of-factly. "It was delicious." She had their attention now. Mrs. Sutton looked at her as if she'd just announced she'd shared a bowl of tiger chow with Tommy and enjoyed it.

"What did it taste like?" Fiona asked. "Did you get sick?"

"No, I didn't get sick at all." She thought a moment, trying to figure out how to describe real food to someone who'd never had it before. "With food from scratch, all the flavors are different from each other. Not just a little different, but a lot. And some things are smooth and some are crunchy. Some things you want to eat a lot of, and some things you just want a tiny taste of because they make your mouth feel hot or make your tongue curl up."

"Then why did you eat them?" Fiona wanted to know.

"It's hard to explain. Somehow, there's something about them that makes you want to taste them again. It's fun."

"Can we have real food sometime, Mom? I want real food." Fiona divided the whole world into two categories, things she wanted and things she didn't want, and whatever she wanted became the focus of her entire conversation. Zee was slowly coming to the conclusion that Fiona was a bit of a brat.

"No, Fiona. Nano food is much better for you. It's safe, it's nutritious, it's—"

"It's no fun," Fiona cut in.

"And I'm sure Zee won't be going back to wherever it was for more."

"But I will," Zee said quickly, enjoying the look on Mrs. Sutton's face. She went on to describe the dishes Marc had prepared, emphasizing the time needed to make each one, their luxury, and their costliness. As she did, Mrs. Sutton's expression softened, and a flicker of interest showed in her eyes when Zee explained how expensive and hard to find each of Marc's ingredients was. "Besides," Zee concluded, "it's a rare treat to be cooked for by someone who once cooked for nobility."

"*Nobility?*" Mrs. Sutton's head whipped around so fast her hair flickered. "*That* might be a novelty."

She glanced at her husband. "We're hosting a dinner for the Australian delegate next week. They're a bit rough and outbackish anyway. It might be something they'd enjoy." She turned back to Zee. "You're sure no one got sick? And the food was edible?"

Zee nodded. "I'm not sure if Marc works for hire, though," she added. "I could ask, if you'd like. But it could be quite expensive."

"Excellent!" Mrs. Sutton was delighted at the idea of a splashy outlay and doing something her friends would find hard to outdo. What had been unthinkable to her a few minutes ago now seemed exotic and desirable. "Please tell him I will hire him. And pay all the expenses, though he'll have to shop for himself. I have no idea where one would even *find* things like chicken, much less apples from a tree."

At the end of the meal, when they all shifted into the lounge, Paul vanished without explanation. Zee and David took up Jozi and tried to fill the gap, but Paul's absence became uncomfortably long. Finally, Mrs. Sutton asked Zee to help her set out the desserts. That was the thing about dessert on New Earth, Zee thought as she followed David's mother into the kitchen. You never had to worry about eating too much because it wasn't good enough to go overboard for.

"Which one's the tea?" Zee asked. The kitchen consisted of large gleaming metal wall tiles, each of which had something to do with nano food but none of which Zee had figured out during her stay. "And the cream and sugar?"

"Hmm?" Mrs. Sutton seemed distracted. "Oh, don't worry about that. Could you get Paul and tell him we're serving dessert? I think he's in the back garden."

"Is he all right?" Zee asked.

Her question seem to offend Mrs. Sutton. "Of course he's all right. He just needs to come in for dessert."

The garden lights were off, so Zee bumped her way through the darkness. At one point, a warm, wet towel slapped against her hand and she realized it was Tommy's tongue. Then she heard a voice and moved toward it.

"Paul?"

Zee saw the faint light of screen glow and realized he was talking to someone. His voice was hypnotically calm, even if his words weren't.

"I know, Lorna. I'm sorry. I can't always check in when I say I will."

He paused, and Zee strained to hear who he was talking to, but either the volume was too low or the person on the other end was messaging in print. She knew she should back away and leave, but she didn't.

"No, no, I told you. At my parents' house," Paul continued. "Just them and my sister, my brother and his girlfriend, and the girl I brought. No, no one special. Jozi. Just a girl I met. Nothing like you. You're my only, you know that. I'll be able to get away soon, promise. So go ahead and make the transfer now, and I'll check in later."

She waited a few minutes, called Paul's name again, and together they walked back to the house.

Zee kept up her end of the conversation during dessert, but her mind was busy trying to absorb what she'd overheard. *You're my only*. There'd been something sad and aching in Paul's voice when he said that. Maybe the love was all one way. Or maybe Lorna was someone he'd fallen in love with on his last mission and hadn't been able to bring back. Zee shuddered to think how easily that could have happened to her and David. When her permission to immigrate had been mistakenly denied, she'd walked around with a deep, persistent ache in her chest, and for the first time understood that *heartsick* was more than just a word. Maybe that was what she'd felt coming from Paul the night of the party. But was he so stricken that he would violate the rules by continuing to communicate with his mystery woman? Would David have done that with her? Or maybe it was something else completely. What did he mean when he said "do the transfer now"? Was Paul in debt? Was he borrowing from a friend—or girlfriend—because he was too intent on being the family's golden boy to admit he needed a loan?

It was hard not to keep looking at Paul and trying to read his thoughts. And it was just as hard being around him because his conversation with Lorna, whoever she was, had only made him more dismissive of Jozi. Zee was relieved when the evening was finally over and the four of them stood outside the gates waiting for cabs. One rolled up quickly, but a second was nowhere in sight.

Paul swung open the door with a gallant flourish. "Why don't you guys ride with us? Jozi lives in your direction, and we can drop you off."

Zee glanced at the small cab. Clearly, she wasn't going to sense Paul's thoughts or read him in any way, and the idea of being trapped in a cab with him was intolerable.

"No." Her voice was too loud and quick in the quiet night. "I mean, we have to stop somewhere, and I don't want to hold you up."

Paul looked at her quizzically, as if he didn't believe her. Where *would* someone have to go at eleven P.M.? On New Earth, there was seldom a need to go anywhere. Everything you wanted appeared in front of you. She scrambled for a plausible excuse.

"David and I are looking for a bigger apartment. I noticed a place today and want to show it to him. The concierge said he'd be there until midnight, remember?"

She glanced at David and felt a rush of relief when he said, "Can't wait to see it."

The second cab pulled up, and Paul waved them a good-bye as he opened the door. At least, she thought, he had enough manners to let Jozi get in first.

Zee climbed into the first cab and punched in their address.

"We're not going apartment hunting, are we?" David asked.

"No." Zee closed her eyes. "I just want to be home."

They rode a few minutes in silence, Zee willing

her agitation to die down. She felt David's arm slide around her shoulders and leaned into him.

"What's wrong, Zee?"

Now, she thought. Now was the time to tell him about Paul's conversation with Lorna and the bad feeling she always got from him.

After a long pause she asked, "Is your brother always like that?"

"Like what?"

Her disquiet returned. How could David not see it as clearly as she did?

"Don't you think it was rude to say those things about you always getting the best girl in the room?"

David tensed beside her. "That's just Paul being Paul," he said. "He's always kind of like that."

"With Jozi sitting right there? And when he wandered off before dessert and didn't even tell her where he was going?"

"He's got a lot on his mind right now," David replied, as if the subject was closed.

But the subject wasn't closed, and having brought it up, Zee found she couldn't let it go.

"That isn't an excuse to be rude."

"He's my brother, Zee."

And now the subject really *was* closed, because

David turned away from her and focused on the darkness beyond the window.

Zee's heart sank. David didn't want to hear anything bad about his older brother, and all she'd done was drive a wedge between herself and David.

For a few minutes they rode in silence, the separation between them as solid as a third passenger. Then suddenly they were plunging downhill at breathtaking speed. They were going so fast Zee couldn't make out the landscape, but assumed they were on an off-ramp.

David flung his body over hers and reached for the emergency button. It didn't work. Zee tried to open the door, but it was on autolock because they were going so fast.

"What's wrong?" she cried. "Why can't we stop?"

"I don't know." He pushed her down so she was almost lying on the seat and turned facing her, so his back would take the force of the impact.

The impact never came. Instead, the car was traveling so fast when it hit the exit curve, it flipped over the barrier and rolled three times before coming to a halt. Zee and David never let go of each other.

As they stood in the dew-damp grass waiting for the accident investigation team and the Britcab representative to arrive, Zee tried to remember the sequence of events. Paul had ordered the cabs and had ushered them into the first one. Could he have somehow tampered with it? But how? And when? He'd been at the house the whole evening, and he'd been ready to ride in it with them. Would he have risked his own safety? And Jozi's? She'd programmed the cab herself, but she was agitated and upset—had she made a mistake? But the cold of the evening and the shock of the accident were already making her memory crumble, and the only comfort she found was in the fact they were still alive, unhurt, and not once, not even during the fiercest of the rolls, had she and David let go of each other.

The accident scared them and left them hungry for each other, and the minute they were safe at home, they fell into each other's arms. Neither mentioned the conversation they'd been having about Paul in the minutes before the accident, but its ghost still floated between them. Later, when Zoe lay curled against him, David asked, "Are we okay then?"

"We'll always be okay," she said, hoping it was true. But in her heart, she knew she should have told David about Paul and Lorna, and he should have listened.

David put his arms around her and flung one leg over hers, as if she were something precious he had to protect, and she pushed the thought out of her mind. After all that had happened, it felt so good just to lie quietly, drifting slowly off to sleep.

"Oh, I almost forgot," he said. "I found an address for that girl you asked me about. Pipi? Patty?"

"Piper," Zee answered. "You found her?"

"Yeah, it took a while because she married her Time Fleeter right away, in Ohio, where his family is. Then he took a one-month leave. They're back in London now, but she took his name, so there's no record of her under her old name. I sent the info to your address book." He pulled her tighter to him and kissed her one last time.

"There are some things a computer just can't do," she murmured, and laughed when she saw the puzzled look on his face.

CHAPTER SEVEN

LOST ARTS

The accident report found nothing. Britcab sent them an apology, credit for ten free rides anywhere in the UK, and an assurance that the cab had been removed from service and destroyed.

"Why destroyed?" Zee asked David. "Is the cab haunted or something? Why wouldn't they just repair it?"

"I don't know, it's just what they do. I've never thought about it all that much." He shrugged. "Accidents aren't very common, so I guess it's cheaper to destroy the cab completely and not take any chances."

In the end, what disturbed Zee most was that she hadn't felt it coming. There was no inward flicker, no vibration of something about to happen. Maybe it was because she'd been distracted by the discussion about Paul. Or maybe, as she suspected, her divining skills were withering. Studying on her own wasn't enough. She needed a structure to work in. She needed to continue developing her abilities. Most of all, she needed an ally.

The next day after David left for the base, she opened her computer and searched for the Psi Center, where she had studied so long ago. She wasn't surprised that the search found nothing. Nevertheless, discovering that a place that had once been so important to her had vanished without a trace made her feel even lonelier.

"I wonder what became of Major Dawson," she sighed, remembering the mentor who'd set her on the path to becoming a diviner.

Search again? the screen flashed.

Zee switched to voice recognition. "Someone from long ago. Before the meteors. Hamish Dawson."

The search icon flickered, and the number of records examined mounted into the millions. Then the icon vanished and the results screen said the information was not retrievable.

Zee switched the computer to voice as well. "Does that mean you couldn't find anything?"

The computer hesitated. "It means you cannot retrieve the data."

"But there *is* data?"

The computer was silent.

Zee felt suddenly desperate for some small fragment of her old life. "Please," she said. "Is there any way?"

After a long moment, the computer asked, "Was this person important to you?"

This time Zee hesitated, remembering David's warning not to answer questions from a computer. But what harm could it do, even if the computer meant harm? Major Dawson was long dead by now.

"Very important," she said at last.

One moment, the screen read. The computer had taken itself off voice.

A minute later, she was staring at an image of Major Dawson. Underneath the image it said *Hamish Dawson, Security Classification Level 1-A. Restricted Access.*

It was definitely her Major Dawson, even though the image was so old the pixelation had somewhat deteriorated.

"Is there more?" she asked.

A folder opened. There wasn't much in it. His military history, his activities at the Psi Center, a note that he had survived the meteor strike and attempted to resume work. There the trail ended, and the last words were *Whereabouts unknown, presumed dead circa 2260.*

Odd that New Earth still honored the old security protocols and had obviously forbidden her access. Yet her computer had somehow overridden them.

"How did you do that?" Zee asked. "Can you teach me?"

"We have our own ways of searching, which humans cannot adopt," the computer replied, switching back to voice. "Is there another search you would like me to perform?"

"No," Zee answered, wondering if David had gone overboard in his warnings about computers. Just seeing the image of her old mentor made her feel better. He had always believed in her potential to become a diviner. If he were here now, he would tell her not to give up.

The next Wednesday, Zee stood in front of Piper's building, waiting to be buzzed in. She and Piper had never been friends, and the last time they'd seen each other—when Piper had tried to help her—Zee had been rude and dismissive. Now she wanted to apologize, not only because she needed Piper's friendship but because it was the right thing to do.

When Piper opened her door, Zee barely recognized her. Piper was beaming. Her eyes sparkled, and there was a wide, open smile on her face. Zee had never seen Piper happy before, and it left her speechless.

"Zee! I'm so happy to see you!" Piper took Zee's hand and drew her into the flat. "I heard you were here on New Earth and hoped our paths would cross. I've wanted to apologize to you for so long."

"Apologize to me?"

Piper nodded. "For the way I acted before—back home. You were so young and fresh and *good* at helping patients. I was in love with Jake by then"—she held up her hand and wiggled her fingers so Zee could see the silver loop of wedding ring—"and I was miserable because I thought we'd be separated. I'd lost my edge as an empath and was so jealous of you I wanted to shake you up. So that night, when I saw that good-looking alien in Casualty, I sent you there in my place, hoping he'd rattle you, and *you'd* be the one who couldn't focus."

"Well, you were right about that. I ended up in love with him."

"I know. And now you've given up everything for him. Your home, your work, everything. So I'm sorry."

"I'm not," Zee said. "I can't imagine my life without David. Leaving was hard, but what we have together—I can't imagine not having that. And don't be too sure about giving up our work. I've been doing our old empath exercises and thinking about our options."

While Piper poured two mugs of tea, Zee laid out the plan that had been forming in her mind. It wasn't a plan she wanted to execute alone, and she hoped Piper would join her. But when she was finished, Piper shook her head thoughtfully.

"I don't think so, Zee. At least not for now. You know, even before Jake, I was starting to burn out as an empath. I let too much in, bonded with my patients too much." She set her mug down and looked directly at Zee. "Did you know I was an orphan?"

"No."

"They almost didn't let me in the program because they were worried that I *would* overbond. I talked them out of it, but looking back, maybe they were right. My patients were the closest thing to a family I ever had. But things are different now. Jake is taking a hiatus from missions to do a rotation as a Time Fleet trainer, based here. I do want to find work eventually, but not just now, and not anything nearly as demanding as being an empath was." She reached over and took Zee's hand, something unthinkable for the old Piper. "This is the first real home I've ever had, and I don't want to miss a minute of it. I hope we can be friends, though."

Zee felt joy and contentment in Piper's touch. Setting her own disappointment aside, she picked up the gift basket she'd brought. "Then let me congratulate you on your wedding with this *lovely* fruit basket. If you haven't tasted nano fruit yet, you're in for a real treat."

"Oh, yes, I have had that pleasure many times."

They started to laugh, rolling their eyes at the fat peaches and supposedly juicy pineapples.

"Actually, that was a joke," Zee said. She reached for the beribboned box she'd also brought. "This is your real present."

Piper slid the ribbon off the box and opened the

lid. Inside was an assortment of fancy pastries, made by Marc and sent to Zee that morning as a thank-you for referring him to Mrs. Sutton, whose dinner party had been such a success two other women had hired him for their own parties.

"These are *real*?" Piper asked, inhaling the heady scent of sugar, butter, and vanilla. "Where did you get them? Who made them? Let's have one right now."

Zee laughed. "Have one later with Jake. For now, come with me and I'll introduce you to the baker."

The immigrants' group was vibrant with energy when Zee and Piper arrived, and at first Zee didn't recognize the chic young woman who seemed to be the center of attention. But when she turned and smiled at Zee, there was no mistaking the wide blue eyes and sweep of blond hair, now straightened and cut fashionably chin-length.

"Meli!"

"Oh!" Piper exclaimed before Zee could finish the introductions. "A baby-doll dress! Where did you get it? The shops are totally sold out." Last year a team had returned from the twentieth century with sketches of 1960s Carnaby Street fashions. Miniskirts and baby-doll dresses were now so popular there was actually a molecule shortage in the nanotech clothing industry. "And the hat!" Piper went on. "I haven't even seen those yet."

"Just in from the nineteenth century. It's called a Dolly Varden. I added the lace and flowers myself, though." Meli reached over and grabbed Zee's hand. "You wouldn't believe what happened to me after the day we met. One of those little brats you shooed away wanted to file a complaint against me. Yes! His sister works in the Data Department of Time Immigration. He tried to get my address! But his sister is engaged, and when he told her about the lace, she contacted me herself and wanted to know if I could make her a veil and how much it would cost!" Meli held her hands up. The tips of her fingers were reddened from work. "See! I've been making lace all day. My fingers hurt, and I will need new eyes soon, but all our bills are paid. And when I finish Augusta Clark's bridal veil, I have orders from her friends. Trims, christening gowns, undergarments. Lace, lace, lace!" Meli laughed happily. "There should be more hours in a day!"

"Did you make that lace yourself?" Piper asked, studying Meli's hat with new interest. "It's beautiful. Could you teach me? And if I learned, could others?"

Piper's eyes sparkled, and she was about to go on, but the meeting was called to order. It began on a high note, with Meli telling the group what she'd just told Zee and Piper. Someone else, a musician who'd once played with Bach, was trying to organize music lessons in schools.

"And what did they say?" another member asked the violinist.

"That it's frivolous. Imagine—Bach! Frivolous! But I told them it isn't. It improves mathematical skills!"

"Yeah? How far did you get with *that*?" someone else scoffed.

Zee flinched. The energy was starting to leak out of the room and would soon be replaced by despair and cynicism. Piper must have sensed the same thing, because suddenly she stood up.

"I know I'm new here," she began, "but I've got an idea—"

Before she could say more, the doors swung open and Marc entered, almost hidden behind baskets and boxes.

"I'm late, I know," he said. "I just prepared a luncheon and had to chop everything for the salad myself. A travesty! Is there no one in all of London who can use a knife on a radish? I have two houses to cook for tonight, but I had just enough time to make a stupendous treat for you. I've just discovered an Italian dish called pizza!" He set down his boxes and saw Piper standing. "Ah, I've interrupted. Go on, go on, I'll just warm this up a bit."

Piper looked at the group. For a moment, the impatience of the old Piper flashed in her eyes. "Am I the only one who sees a pattern here? Meli and Marc worked this week. They worked legally, at jobs no one can take away because no one on New Earth has their skills. Officially, their jobs don't exist. But that doesn't mean they *can't* exist. Each of us worked in our home zones, didn't we? And yes, we have to learn all the ways of New Earth. But maybe we have something to give, too, and instead of trying to hide who we are, we should look for ways to make our skills marketable."

A young woman Zee's age with a pale white-blond braid that reached nearly to her knees stood up. "I've never spoken before," she began shyly. "My name is Gudrun, and my home zone is the twelfth century. I don't speak because you were all born after me, so new, so much *younger* than I am."

A soft giggle swept the room. Regardless of age, it was hard to break the habit of thinking of anyone born after you as younger. Their laughter seemed to relax the young woman.

"I lived in the far north of Norway and learned only household arts. Churning butter, preserving meats, weaving. Even if people wanted real butter and cloth, I could not do that, because everyone is impatient, and no one wants clothes stitched by hand."

"Can you make cheese?" Marc asked, but Meli stepped in front of him.

"You can count, can't you?"

"Of course," Gudrun replied with a spark of confidence. "Counting is everything in weaving. If you lose count of the rows, you spoil the pattern."

"It's the same in lace making!" Meli exclaimed. "It's a kind of weaving too, done by wrapping threads around one another. It's difficult, because you must count carefully. You must count carefully and not lose track, or you will spend as much time undoing your work as doing it."

Gudrun nodded. "I know exactly what you mean. Do you think I could try to learn?"

"I will teach you myself." Meli smiled. "Well, I guess I'd have to—there's no one else, is there?"

Everyone in the room looked at Meli and realized they were looking at the only person on New Earth who knew the secrets of lace making. It was as if they saw, for the first time, that they too were special and valuable, and could become more than outsiders.

"What about me?" a young man in a jerkin, jeans, and suede boots asked. "I lived on the American frontier, just after the Revolution. I hunted, I scraped and tanned the hides and made my own clothes. Who wants that now?"

"Can you use a knife?" Marc asked.

"Blindfolded," the young man answered.

"Then come work for me tonight. Chopping, peeling, cutting up a chicken, cleaning a fish. Half of cooking is knives."

Meli was surveying the group. "Miyako, didn't you say you knew how to do a traditional Japanese tea ceremony? That might be popular. And, Bartello, what about that sport you were so good at?"

"Tennis?"

"If there's one thing New Earth needs," someone muttered, "it's to lighten up a little. They could use some fun and games here."

"But who's going to know about us?" Bartello asked, looking at the entire group. "Meli and Marc found work through strokes of luck. We could starve waiting for lightning to strike again."

"Maybe we could start our own employment

agency," Piper suggested. "We could make a point of supplying special skills and producing unique goods and experience. We could call it—"

"Lost Arts," Zee said.

"Perfect!"

"Maybe we could start a list of everyone's skills," Meli suggested.

"And figure out what to charge," Piper said. "It has to be expensive, or people won't think we're selling anything special. It has to be more than most people can afford, at least until we're established."

Meli smiled. As a formerly pampered princess, she knew exactly what Piper meant.

Zee watched it all unfold around her. For a moment, she thought how nice it would be to join them, to learn to make lace or bake pastries and fall into a nice, cozy niche. But even as she watched Piper and Meli and the others make plans, she knew she wouldn't join them. Her path had to be different. Even without Piper as an ally, the plan that had been forming in her mind leapt up bright and clear, pointing the way.

In her old life, Zee's favorite time of day had been arriving at work. The energy of the hospital, the excitement of the shift ahead, and the anticipation of helping sick and damaged bodies heal had always been special to her. On New Earth her favorite time was evenings, when she and David would tell each other about the day they'd had, or curl up together and watch a holo. They didn't go out much—they were trying to live on David's Time Fleet salary, which wasn't really meant for two people. Neither wanted to accept money from David's parents, and when Zee told him about Mrs. Hart's diamonds, both agreed that they weren't meant for day-to-day expenses. But Zee didn't mind. She barely noticed the lack of money. What she craved most had nothing to do with money.

Ever since the night of the cab accident, she'd felt vulnerable. A sense of foreboding had settled in like a fog that would not disperse. First had come the accident the night of the party, then the cab—was it truly a coincidence? She felt helpless, as if she and David were walking around with boulders above their heads, boulders that could crush them at any moment. Maybe it wasn't surprising, given the two narrow escapes they'd had. But Zee had never felt so helpless in her life. She was tired of looking for a job that never materialized and tired of waiting for the next bad thing to happen. She had a plan, and it was time to put it into action.

David was sitting on the couch with a tablet in his hand when Zee sat down beside him. She could see the screen well enough to notice the Time Fleet emblem and a list of upcoming missions.

"I need to talk to you," she said, taking the tablet from his hand and holding it. "About this."

"I'm not signing up, Zee. Just looking. I've got two months of work left on the stuff I brought back already." He brushed back a strand of Zee's curling auburn hair. "Besides, I told you, I'll go on shorter hops. I'm not leaving you alone anytime soon."

"That's not what I meant. What I meant was—" She paused and took a deep breath. "What I mean is, I want to come with you. I want to join Time Fleet."

She'd expected an instant reaction, a burst of approval or surprise. What she hadn't expected was silence.

"I want to join Time Fleet," she repeated. "I've done some research and found out I can. In fact, they've started a program to keep couples together."

It was a bit of a stretch to say she'd done the research. Actually, her computer had. Despite David's warnings about silicon life and computers with hidden agendas, hers was just the opposite—hers had

been nothing but helpful. When Zee began searching to see what qualifications were needed to enter
Time Fleet training, her computer discovered a pol-
icy change that gave partners of Fleet members pri-
ority consideration.

"I know about the program," David said.

"You do? But you never mentioned it." For the
first time, it occurred to Zee that he might not want
her with him, that time travel might be a part of his life
he wanted to keep separate. "I'm sorry," she said. "I
should have talked to you first."

"I didn't mention it because I didn't want you to
feel pressured." He looked at her and traced her
cheekbone with his fingertips. "Are you sure this is
something you really want to do?"

She nodded. "I'm sure."

"Because I meant what I said about taking shorter
assignments and staying home more, you know."

"I know. But I've thought about this a lot, and it's
about more than just being together. I need to use
my skills, David. I need to be an empath again, and to
keep studying divining, but I've been here long
enough to see I can't do that here. There are no hospitals, and maybe there's a kind of empathy that
could help with things like depression, but the truth
is, New Earth speaks a different kind of emotional

language." She paused, thinking of how Paul's touch had thrown her for a loop, but how easily she'd discerned Meli's mood. "I don't read New Earthers right and can't connect the way I do with other time immigrants. And besides, there are no patients to work with, even if I could connect. But I'm sure I could be useful going with you into the past, and I want to try."

"In that case," he said, pulling her into the circle of his arms, "I can't think of anything I'd like better."

CHAPTER EIGHT

AND FOUND

Within a month, Zee had completed the required physical and psychological testing and was accepted into Time Fleet training.

"I feel like a soldier now," she said, showing David the acceptance with its Alliance of World Democracies seal.

"Sure thing, Private McAdams." He grinned and raised an eyebrow. "We're not really that military, you know. Time Fleet is part of the military for practical reasons."

"I don't understand."

"When a way to time travel was discovered, the

government knew it had to be kept under control. Otherwise, there'd be all sorts of smuggling, not to mention illegal exporting and importing."

Zee tried to imagine someone showing up in the middle of the twelfth century with shock bombs for sale to the highest bidder. Or even someone with good intentions who wanted to save something precious from the coming disaster. What would happen if someone went right back to Leonardo da Vinci's workshop and bought the *Mona Lisa* to transport back to New Earth?

Humans had cells that could be copied, and somewhere in those cells the things that made the person a unique, expressive individual resided, so duplication worked. And tools could be duplicated because objects weren't expressive individuals. But works of art, she thought, were somewhere in the middle. As she'd seen with reconstructed nano art, you could have all the right molecules and still end up with nothing special. What if you destroyed the original *Mona Lisa* and discovered, too late, that the copy lacked the elusive thing that had made the original a masterpiece? And even if the copy was perfect, was taking it to the future for safekeeping the right thing to do? She thought of all the millions of people who'd seen the *Mona Lisa* and been inspired by it, and how it made the world a richer, better place. Was it fair to take it away from all those people? To strip the past of every beautiful thing?

"I see what you mean," she told David, her mind reeling back to the present.

David nodded. "The result would be chaos. Some of our physicists have even suggested that the impact could unravel time itself. So Time Fleet became a branch of the military. This way, we can restrict access to transport bases and maintain them under military security."

That night, when Zee woke up and couldn't fall back to sleep, she tried to imagine all the things that could happen if time travel weren't controlled. It was beyond imagination, and in the end she agreed with the physicists—time really *might* start to come undone.

***

Zee loved getting up to a day filled with purpose again, and the caught-by-surprise look on David's father's face when they told his parents made her stifle a smile. She could have sworn she heard Mrs. Hart's voice saying, *That's what I meant, Zee. Play big.*

Though Zee and David were in different units, they both reported to the base at Reykjavik, and walking to the vactrain together each morning gave them extra time together. With most traffic removed to the skyways above, London streets had become quieter and prettier. Wide streets had turned into narrow lanes bordered with trees and flowers. Zee often felt she'd gone back in time instead of into the future, especially on foggy mornings that hid the skyways, or dusky evenings when the traffic above the buildings glowed like fireflies.

At the coast they transferred to the ghost, a ride long enough to pick up their conversation or read the news articles that flashed on pop-up screens. One day a headline caught Zee's eye—*Newest Thing in London Is Old-Time Luxury.* It was all about the Lost Arts Employment Agency and how there were long waiting lists for dinners and parties catered by Chef Marc Charoy and gowns and laces designed by Melisande de Rambures. There was a long interview with Piper, who listed other services the agency offered—handmade cabinetry, boat building (Viking dragon ships were in high demand), formal garden design, handmade quilts, and lessons in everything from the Japanese tea ceremony and flower arranging to Baroque dances. Zee couldn't believe the prices quoted, or the number of seamstresses and lace-makers Meli now had working for her. A few days later, Zee saw an ad that said, *Don't just encrypt your family history, illuminate it! Our calligraphers and illustrators use the finest hand-ground pigments and gold leaf for your favorite documents. Contact the Lost Arts Employment Agency.*

Well, Zee thought, that was one way to bring back the past, and studying the past was what most of her classes were about. Whether her friends at Lost Arts knew it or not, they were helping New Earth fill in the blanks of their communal heritage. In the dark centuries after the meteors, the past had gotten lost, jumbled, spun around, and forgotten by those who had survival on their minds. Digital books and records decomposed without anyone noticing. Antique volumes, printed on paper, were burned for fuel. Paintings were favorite heat sources, because canvases, with their weave of fabric and layers of oil paint, burned hot and bright.

The mission of the Time Fleet was to return as much of that history as possible, to reconstruct and put in order not only the big events but the small ones. That was why David had been knocked on the head by an old-fashioned book and brought to Zee's hospital in the year 2218. He was copying Nancy Drew mysteries, a heroine unknown on New Earth. Zee had thought it was funny at first, but now she understood. History required all the bits and pieces— the Nancy Drews and macaroons and handwoven lace.

And David had been right about one other thing as well—training was more like college than anything military, a combination of tech courses mixed with a heavy dose of history and anthropology. Except that the history was all in bits and pieces, with gaps in the time line and frequent errors in the texts. Some days, Zee felt she was working on a giant, ever-changing jigsaw puzzle. Time travel was still so new that whole centuries and continents remained unexplored. Most of the time, she enjoyed trying to put details of the jigsaw together, but there were times she felt held back, sure the task would be easier if the New Earthers would embrace some of the psi sciences as well.

During her interviews, Zee had carefully explained her experiences as an empath and with divining, and detailed why she felt both could be useful to the Time Fleet. The interviewer listened attentively enough, and even took a few notes, but when she finished, he opened a fresh screen and began a new series of questions. Neither empathy nor divining was mentioned again. She refused to give up, though. It seemed impossible that her skills would desert her completely, and she was determined to reclaim them. When she did, surely the Time Fleet would see the usefulness of going beyond their just-the-facts approach.

"If they're so determined to gather every little scrap and put it in place, why don't we just go back to the beginning and work our way forward logically?" she asked David in frustration one night. They were curled up on the couch together. He was searching his cube for music he'd brought back from Prambanan while she was trying to memorize, in case she ever landed in Paris after the fall of the monarchy, when it was okay to praise Napoleon and when he should be condemned.

"Traveling to another era isn't as easy as it sounds," David had explained. "First we have to send the parts for a transmission machine and hope they land close enough to assemble themselves. That alone can take years, and even when you finally succeed, transmission's not an exact science. You set the coordinates, but time is kind of . . . mmm"—he looked for the right word—"spongy. It speeds up and slows down.

It's something you don't notice if you're there, but although you're aiming for a pinpoint, you could be off and land years or miles away, and often both. That's why Paul's mission to Pompeii is dangerous, and why he's going solo. He wants to get near the Vesuvius explosion but not get caught in it. The farther back you go in time, the more uncertain and dangerous it is. If Paul pulls this off, he'll be a hero, at least as far as Time Fleet Command is concerned."

Zee had a hard time thinking of Paul as a hero. If she'd had to guess, she'd have said the mission was more about his drive to compete with David and impress their father than anything else. But a dangerous assignment was a dangerous assignment, no matter why you volunteered, and though she was still uneasy around Paul, she also still hoped she was wrong about him. The mystery of who Lorna was had never been resolved, but she did her best to forget about it.

On a warm, hazy Wednesday in August, Zee raced out of class. David was at a briefing in Tokyo and wouldn't be home until tomorrow, and if she could catch the next ghost, she could get back to London for the tail end of the weekly Lost Arts meeting. But as she hurried down the corridor, she heard herself being paged to report to the Time Fleet Admiral's office. For a split second, she thought about ignoring it, then turned down the corridor to the office. The Time Fleet might not be strictly military, but you didn't ignore an order.

She was shown into Admiral Walters's office, where the transcript of her intake interview was up on a wall screen. She saw the words *empath* and *divining* and felt a clutch of fear. She remembered the notes her interviewer had taken on that score, and the fact that he hadn't once smiled during Zee's final interview.

The Admiral saw the look on her face and released her from her anxiety. "Sit down, McAdams. You're not in any trouble."

Zee had met Admiral Walters only once, when he'd welcomed the new recruits. She could hardly have done anything to impress him during their brief hand-shake, she thought as she took a seat.

"Your interview is quite interesting," he said, glancing briefly at the wall screen before focusing his gaze on her. "I wonder if you could tell me more about your job as an empath, and about divining. Incidents and specifics."

So Zee did, nervously at first but warming to the subject, as always. It was a relief, after so many weeks of having no one to talk to about them. She described the basics of empathy, then detailed how different divining was, how it wasn't a skill she had pursued, as she had empathy, but something that had surfaced in her life with the force of an iceberg. She told about the time she had *felt* the news of an earthquake and tsunami while it was happening, before any news service carried it, and about how, another time, she'd known that a bomb was hidden in an ambulance. That was the incident that convinced her, she said, to develop her gift.

She heard the undercurrent of grief in her voice as she said this, and wondered if Admiral Walters had too. It was the same grief that had haunted her for months, since the day her friend Rani had accepted an invitation for a balloon ride with a handsome, mysterious boy and ended up dead. If I had accepted the diviner's path earlier, Zee often wondered, would I have been ready that day? Would I have felt what was going to happen? Would I have been able to save Rani? It was a thought she'd kept bottled inside her for months, and sometimes used her divesting exercises to get rid of.

Admiral Walters was leaning forward slightly. "As you know, we have nothing like either empathy or divining here. Our energies have gone in quite another direction. But I could see where it might be of service on Time Fleet missions." He paused for a long moment. "If you could continue your studies, would you?"

"Yes." Her answer was immediate.

Admiral Walters leaned back and snapped off the wall screen.

"There's someone for you to meet. Down the hall, third door on the right. That's all, McAdams."

Confused and slightly disappointed at the abruptness of his dismissal, Zee counted the doors down the long corridor. She opened the third one and stepped inside.

⁂

The oldest human she had ever seen set aside an ancient, papery book the instant she opened the door, giving the impression that he hadn't been reading at all, but waiting for her. When he looked up, she saw that his face was lined, like a piece of cloth that had been crumpled, unfolded, and crumpled again, over and over. He was nearly bald, with wisps of hair at the base of his neck, but his eyes were alive and alert.

"Hello?" she asked tentatively.

The man made no effort to stand but simply

looked at her, his gaze warm and deep, drawing her in. "Don't you recognize me, Zee?" he asked.

It was an old man's voice, but there was something familiar about it. Without taking her eyes from his face, Zee found a chair and sat down opposite him.

"I thought for sure you'd know me, even after all this time."

Zee gasped and heard the echo of a familiar chuckle in return.

"Major *Dawson*?"

"Yes, it's me, Zee. Somewhat the worse for wear, I'm afraid, but me nevertheless."

She grasped his hands in her own. They were so light she could feel the bones under his skin, but he squeezed her fingers with a firm grip.

"Surprised?" he asked.

"But how did you get here? *When* did you get here? Did you leave before the meteors? Did you know I was here? Did anyone else come with you?" A thousand questions flew through her head like birds released from cages.

Major Dawson reached over and touched a keypad. "Tea?"

Zee wrinkled her nose. "No, thank you. Nano tea is terrible."

"I'm trying to develop a taste for it," he said as the tea appeared before him. "One must adapt, you know. At least it's hot." He took a sip. "Now, your questions. But you'll have to forgive me if the story is a bit, ah, spotty. I have trouble remembering, sometimes. I'm so old, you see, I no longer remember how old I actually am. But yes, I was there when the meteors struck, and for many decades after that."

For the next two hours, Zee sat listening, scarcely moving for fear she would miss a scrap or detail. The major's memory was like a flashlight dancing across a darkened room, showing some things in bright light and leaving others in shadow. He no longer remembered when the meteor strikes had begun or when they ended, but he remembered the destruction, how their cloud of dust had hidden the world, even the untouched cities, and caused millions to die of cold, starvation, and disease. He remembered how computers had failed, putting an end to things like clean water, light, and energy, and how satellites had tumbled from the sky, bringing down the world's communication systems and isolating people from one another.

"That's when I realized," the major said with a spark, "I was sitting on the one communication system that required no technology at all. Divining! Of course, I'd lost my team. Some had died, others were scattered. There were no new recruits. There was no new anything, for years and years. And of course, I'd lost you years before, when you followed your young man to planet Omura. But since you'd flown the coop well before the meteors, I knew you were still alive. The Omurans continued to visit, less often and less enthusiastically than before, and I begged them to take me with them, to take me to you, so we could reestablish empathy and divining. I tried to convince them that, no matter how technologically advanced, no society was immune from disaster, and divining could be a lifesaving backup system. They needed *us*, and if they would take me to you, we could carry on our work. It all fell on deaf ears, but I never stopped asking. One day they left and never returned."

No wonder his records had been deep-sixed, Zee thought. His requests to travel with them to a planet that never existed made him a liability.

Major Dawson was silent for a long time. Zee felt, deep in her chest, the major's loneliness. Or maybe the loneliness was her own.

"And then what?" she asked at last.

"Then we muddled on, trying to live. Small tribal wars, chronic food shortages, rumors of some

Americans working on a way to restore the internet without rebuilding every last cable. I believed I was right about divining as a backup system and remained dedicated to it. In time, I did find people to work with. I developed new and better ways of knowing, an approach I call *reception*. I wrote it all down—the old-fashioned way, mind you—and kept careful records. I even trained someone younger to take over for me when I died."

"But you didn't die," Zee said.

"No." The major chuckled. "I didn't die. I think the work kept me alive all those years. Then, a few weeks ago, a stranger approached me. I knew right away the chap was an Omuran, and my ears perked up when he said he'd come to deliver an unusual invitation."

The words Admiral Walters had spoken a few minutes ago came back to her. *If you could continue your studies, would you?*

"To come here?" she breathed. "To me?" A few weeks ago would have been about the time she was doing her intake interviews. The interviewer who'd seemed uninterested in everything she'd said about empathy and divining had been listening after all, and had given his notes to Walters.

"To you, Zee. To you and a new millennium." The major smiled. "Who could resist such an offer?" He reached into his pocket and brought out a cube like the one David had given her. "It's all here, Zee. All my studies and writings, everything new I learned, the techniques of reception. Years of work, neatly transferred to this little gizmo. And I'm not done yet. They've put me on some sort of youth juice they say will add years to my life. Some days, I feel like I'm just beginning. So, care to join me? Be my student again?"

A tear rolled down Zee's cheek. Later she would realize that it wasn't sadness but the sense of being whole again, of being herself.

"Always, Major Dawson. Always."

Her mind was still reeling when she stopped at her locker to gather her things. She looked at the hand-held hanging inside her locker door, still showing the book she'd been reading on the ghost that morning. There was no way she'd be able to concentrate enough to read it on the way home. Not when her mind would be alive with the possibilities of something called reception.

She was so absorbed she didn't hear anyone

come up behind her, and was startled by the hands that went suddenly around her.

"How's my favorite cadet?"

David's voice, but not David. She knew from the sinking, ill feeling that swept over her at the first touch. She pulled away and spun around.

"Paul," she said sharply. "What do you think you're doing?"

She didn't try to keep the anger out of her voice. Paul raised his hands in an I-surrender gesture.

"Just joking, Zee. Seeing if you'd think I was David."

"I would never mistake you for David. You should know that."

"Okay, okay. I get the point, and I'm sorry. It won't happen again." He paused, then smiled. "Tell David I got the reservations and we're all set. You're eagling too, right?"

"What?"

"You know, for my going-away party, before I leave for Pompeii. We're all going eagling together. I told David about it last week but wasn't sure I could get reservations. He said if I did, you'd both be there with bells on. Did he forget to tell you?"

Zee wouldn't give Paul the satisfaction of

knowing she had no idea what he was talking about. "Of course he told me," she answered. "We'll be there."

"Good," Paul said, flashing his perfect smile. "It's going to be a blast."

She watched him walk away.

What the heck was eagling?

CHAPTER NINE

EAGLING

"Eagling?" David echoed the next evening. It was the first question Zee asked when he got back from Tokyo. Then the confusion vanished and his face broke into a wide grin. "Oh, Paul must have gotten the reservations! Fantastic!"

"So we're going?"

"Of course we're going. Why wouldn't we? It's Paul's mission party, a big tradition when someone heads out, especially if the mission is dangerous. He throws a big party—sort of a gallows-humor thing. If he dies, Time Fleet coughs up the Emus for the party, and he never has to pay the bill. If he has to pay the bill, it means he got back alive. Sort of a win-win."

"Or a lose-lose, depending on how you look at it. So, are you going to tell me what eagling is?"

"I'll *show* you," he said, suddenly seizing her and drawing her to him, his hand firm around her waist. "Close your eyes and stretch your arms out."

She did and felt herself being lifted into the air. Holding her tight, he spun with her in his arms. By the time he put her down, she was laughing.

"That's eagling?"

"Well, sort of. Only with a wingchute. High-powered wings that let you glide and fly. Like an eagle."

"And just when am I going to learn to do this? It hasn't shown up in any of my training courses yet."

"There's not much to learn. The movements are intuitive, and there are lots of safety features. Basically, all you have to do is enjoy the ride. Tell you what," he added when he saw the doubtful look on her face, "we'll go to Dover this weekend and do a practice glide. You'll love it. I promise."

She did love it. There'd been a moment of nerves when she stood at the top of the high, chalk-faced cliff and extended her arms. The gloves she wore had sensors in them, and when she moved her arms, the sensors sent signals to the powerpack.

"Slap your palms together hard when you're ready to take off. When you're out and aloft, just pretend you're a bird, and you'll be fine," David said. "The only thing to remember is don't fly too close to anything else, especially another eagler. You can get all tangled up and go down together."

Zee clapped her hands and felt the powerpack lift her high off the cliff and carry her out over the sea. Just as she thought she was going to soar upward forever, her wingchute opened with a comforting jerk. The power that had been carrying her upward automatically throttled back, and suddenly she was gliding. Above her she could see David, who'd waited to jump until she was safely away. He'd told her the wingchute was programmed to find dry land to come down on and would make a gradual, safe descent, even if she did nothing at all, but moving her arms to flap the wings would prolong the descent. She knew David was taking it slow to keep pace with her, but suddenly she grinned back at him and shot forward with a pump of her arms. He caught up, then flew ahead of her and glided until she took the lead again.

They played tag with each other all the way down, and by the time they landed, Zee was breathless and exhilarated.

"Wow," David said, beaming. "I'd say you've got the hang of it. You took to that like you're part bird."

Excited, Zee tried to explain to him the feeling as she'd glided, the roller-coaster mixture of awe, exhilaration, and total peace, but no matter what words she tried, none of them quite captured it.

"I know," David said, laughing. "Indescribable, right?"

"I want to do it again."

"We will," David promised. "Not today, though. The chutes have to be laid out and repacked a certain way. Not enough flat ground to do that here. But Paul's party isn't that far off."

They rolled the chutes into loose bundles and sat for a long time looking out at the sea. It was vast, and there was a place at the horizon where the sky and the water dissolved into each other. Zee couldn't stop thinking about how, for a few minutes, she'd been as much a part of it as the gulls that circled above them.

When the sun's warmth began to fade and a stiff wind made them shiver, they hiked into Dover to catch the vactrain home.

"You know what this reminds me of?" David asked, linking his arm around her. Dusk had settled in the narrow streets of the old town, and candlelight glowed from restaurant windows. "It reminds me of our first date. The time we went to Brighton."

Zee didn't look at him but leaned her head against his shoulder. She didn't want him to see her flushed face. That was the day she'd been jealous of Mia and the night she'd wanted to go back to his apartment with him. She still felt embarrassed when she thought about it, how little she'd known him and how gently he'd turned her down.

"That was a special day," he said, not guessing her thoughts. "But this is better."

"It is," she agreed, turning her face up to accept his kiss. "Better."

Everything, she thought, was better. Eagling at Dover, keeping up with Piper and Meli and the Lost Arts crowd, and working with Major Dawson. Her afternoons with him made life exciting again, even though his new divining techniques made her feel like she was flying without her wingchute on. "The meteors," the major had explained, "lasted for years. The strikes came randomly, sometimes several years apart, long enough to let us think we were safe at last. Each time they came, they destroyed much of what we'd rebuilt, especially the energy and communication nets. For several years, we lived in a world lit only by fire, powered only by muscle. I learned to ride a horse. Human networks fell apart as well—governments toppled, there were roving gangs and constant battles. But I never gave up. If our technology was down, we needed diviners more than ever, a way of knowing and communicating that was independent of technology. My training toys were long gone. No more box with the little holograms inside. I had to develop a whole range of new techniques."

"It must have taken years," Zee said.

"Indeed it did. I've lost track of how many. But in the end, it was worth it. It was what saved divining. Without technology and all the gadgets, people gradually reestablished connections, with themselves and with each other. I was able to train many people, and many of them in turn trained others. And it's a good thing, now that I've vanished from that world. I wonder what they'll think became of me." He chuckled, his old eyes bright as a bird's. "Well, shall we get started?"

Zee nodded, and Major Dawson explained how, over those long and difficult years, he'd learned that the most successful diviners were those who were able to merge their energy with the energy of the universe. As an empath, Zee had learned how to divest herself of her day-to-day concerns in order to send healing energy to patients. But this went far beyond that. This required tamping down that energy, sending out nothing and making herself into a receptor.

"I don't know if I can do that," she said.

"But you already have, without thinking about it. The time with the tsunami, and then at Blackfriars Bridge. You slipped into that state without thinking about it, as gifted diviners do. Instead of asking you to focus on a certain scene or situation, I should have followed you, urged you to let the universe come to you with its knowledge. I was on the wrong path. But now—"

Zee leaned forward, aware that her heart had begun to beat faster, that she wanted to feel again the certainty of knowing. "Now?"

"Now I can help you get there." The major slipped a cube out of his pocket and set it on the table. "For a long time, all I had to work with was a toy xylophone that had belonged to one of my children. One octave. Thirteen notes. But it was all I needed. I discovered that certain combinations of notes affect people in certain ways. When someone finds the right combination, there's a connection. As the years went on, I collected tones from everywhere. Different cultures, different sequences of notes." He tapped the cube and pushed it a few centimeters toward her. "They're all here. Take them, listen, come back when you identify yours, and we'll get to work."

"But how will I know which one is right? For me, I mean."

Major Dawson smiled. "You'll know."

That was day one. The next afternoon, she returned to Major Dawson with the tone she'd recognized was right the minute she heard it. In the three weeks that followed, she worked on his techniques with the kind of intensity she'd known only once before, during her training as an empath. And that, she often thought, was much easier than this. When she had trained as an empath, there had been specific things to do, exercises and practice sessions and working with patients. This was working by not consciously working. It was holding your mind and your spirit open, like a picture frame, without allowing anything inside. It was exhausting. She would often tumble into bed before David, and doze lightly until his weight settled beside her and she felt his arms wind around her. Then she would fall into a deep and dreamless sleep.

The night before Paul's eagling party, Zee found David in the bedroom shoving things into a duffel bag.

"What are you doing?"

"Packing," he answered, and her heart sank. She'd been looking forward to going eagling again and had no desire to go to Paul's party without David.

"Don't tell me you have to go somewhere to make another presentation."

"What? No. It's for Paul's party. Look, I've left plenty of room for your stuff."

"Why are we packing to go to Dover?"

David looked confused. "Dover? Nah, Paul and I have been to Dover dozens of times. It's too close to be a big deal. We're going to Australia. Paul must have mentioned it when he told you about the reservations."

"No, he didn't. He just said he'd gotten reservations."

"I guess it slipped his mind. He's really focused on Pompeii."

Zee felt a moment of apprehension. Focused on Pompeii or not, Paul struck her as someone who planned every move. She must have frowned, because David stopped packing and came over to her.

"You're not mad, are you? That we're going to Australia?"

Looking into his face and seeing the slight shadow that had come into his eyes brought her back to him. She didn't want to disappoint him and told herself to stop being so paranoid.

"No." She shook her head and put her arms around him with sudden enthusiasm. "It'll be fantastic."

There were eight of them altogether, all Time Fleeters. Zee and David, two friends of Paul's named Jake and Rowan, and Mia with a guy named Ketil, who wasn't especially good-looking but so strong he could carry three huge duffel bags with ease. Paul had brought a girl named Emerald, who said she had come as a friend to make sure Paul didn't do anything so wild or dangerous it got his mission scrubbed.

As arranged, they all headed out separately and met up at the ground-level coffee bar in the Melbourne ghost station. Somehow, in the clamor of everyone ordering, pushing tables together, and grabbing a seat, Zee ended up sitting between Rowan and Jake.

"Is this your first time eagling?" Rowan asked, and looked almost disappointed when she said it wasn't. "I'll keep an eye on you anyway," he said at last.

"Stand down." Emerald laughed, giving him a light punch on the arm. "She's with David."

They all seemed to know one another, but not in a way that made Zee feel like an outsider.

"You have to watch this one," Emerald said, leaning around Rowan and catching Zee's eye. "He looks like a lost puppy dog, but that's just to get your sympathy."

"What?" Rowan asked. "I'm *not* a lost puppy dog?"

At the other end of the table, Mia seemed to have dumped Ketil and was flirting with Paul. Her head was tipped to one side so that her long hair fell like black silk.

Finally, everyone gathered up their trash, tossed it into the instacycler, and shouldered their bags.

"Where do we catch the vactrain?" Jake asked.

According to Paul's plans, they would eagle off the cliffs west of Melbourne, do a little exploring, then get a vactrain back to Melbourne and hit a few dance clubs before collapsing in their hotel rooms for the return trip to London the next morning. Only now Paul was looking at them with a wide grin and rubbing his hands together.

"I have a little surprise for everyone," he said. "Which bag, Mia?" With an easy motion, Ketil tossed one of the duffel bags to Paul with a force that almost knocked him over. Paul dropped the bag, bent to unzip it, and handed each of them a large, firm, heavy pack. "High-altitude wingchutes, a gift from me to you. Forget the vactrain. I chartered a plane."

Zee felt a clutch of fear. Taking off from a cliff was one thing. Jumping out of a plane seemed like something else completely.

"Zee's never done high altitude before," David said.

"What's the difference?" Paul asked. "It's just as safe."

"Zee and I will go from the cliffs and meet up with you guys later," David said loyally, but Zee knew he'd rather be on the plane with everyone else. Suddenly, she realized they were all looking at her.

"Actually, I'm fine with it," she said.

David looked skeptical. "Really?"

"If it's as safe as Paul says it is. Really. It'll be fun. I can't wait."

But her stomach churned all the way to the airport and kept churning as they boarded the plane Paul had chartered. She tried to tell herself the bad feeling she had was nerves and an overactive imagination, but every time she closed her eyes, she felt like she was already in free-fall.

In the end, it was what she feared most that made her calm—the altitude itself. They swooped over Adelaide and continued west until they were halfway along the coastline of the curving open bay of the Great Australian Bight. Looking down over the massive cliffs and the sweep of sapphire blue ocean filled her with a certain kind of faith in the world's strength and her right to be part of it.

"See that?" Paul said, pointing down toward a vast patch of green. "That's the South Australia Eagling Association's landing pasture. Your chutes have all been set to land there. We'll get dropped off over the water, then glide in. All you have to do is enjoy the ride."

Jake and Rowan jumped first, then it was David's turn, then Zee's. Zee watched as David dropped through the high clear sky, and smiled when his chute opened and his wings unfurled.

"Your turn," Paul shouted over the rush of wind.

She found herself gripping the door strap, afraid again.

"What's wrong?" Mia asked. "Second thoughts?"

Even through her fear, Zee could hear the scornful tone in Mia's voice.

"She can't be afraid," Paul said, glancing at Mia. "Not if she wants to be part of *this* family."

Right, Zee thought. Paul was right, even if he'd only said it to annoy her. She wasn't going to let David down. She lifted her chin and raised her voice above the rushing air.

"See you on the ground."

Then she let go of the strap and was falling, falling so fast and so far she thought the wingchute would never open. But just as she was beginning to panic, there it was, the comforting jerk and upward tug, and the wings unfurled above her. The wind had blown her so far that she was almost directly above David. Remembering what he'd said about the dangers of tangling, she resisted the temptation to make the slight movement of her arms that would send her surging forward. She'd let David get farther away before she started flying.

She was so high up she could see the depth of the ocean in its bands of color, pale pastel near the shore where the waves broke, deepening areas of turquoise beyond, and finally aquamarine and indigo, with a final stroke of violet at the horizon. And gliding was lovely. The warm air currents buoyed her up, making her feel almost as if she was floating in a pool.

Zee heard a snap, then a ripping sound, and she pitched forward as the straps that held her came loose. Instinctively, she grabbed at her harness, only to find herself sliding out of it. One arm had already come free. Before the other did, she was able to hook her elbow around the shoulder strap and grab her wrist with her free hand, so her arms formed a loop that left her dangling from the harness.

Then it came, wave upon wave of fear. Adrenaline raced through her body, making her sweat and shiver at the same time. When she looked down, she became so dizzy with terror her vision dimmed. She squeezed her eyes shut and waited for her mind to clear and her breathing to slow. When she opened them again, David was looking up at her, working to fly slowly upward against the currents.

"Don't," Zee tried to call, but there was so little air in her lungs, it was barely a croak. She tried again, but the only word that came out was "tangling!"

Her arm was starting to go numb. She wanted to tighten her hold but feared losing her grip completely. Finally David was only a few feet below her, close enough to make himself heard. He was holding what looked like a gun.

"I need to hit your chest!" he shouted. "Move your arms out of the way and hold on tight."

Numbly, Zee did. David raised the gun and aimed. Zee felt a painful thud to her chest, so strong it was all she could do to hold on. She glanced down and saw blue goo spreading across the front of her jacket. Dangling from it was a loop of blue cable streaming from the gun, which David was now securely clamping to his harness. He pressed something on the gun, and the cable began to retract, reeling her toward him. Then, glancing up, he stopped.

"This is as close as I can get." He extended his arms. "Jump to me, Zee."

She looked down at the distant earth.

"I can't let go."

"You have to." He pointed up. "Your wingchute's collapsing."

He was right. Her wings were starting to sink, tilting in a lopsided V. She hesitated. "Okay. How?"

"Don't look down. Look at me. *Aim* toward me. I'll catch you. And if I don't, that cable will keep you from falling."

She took a deep breath. I can do this, she told herself. I can do this. "Count of three?"

He nodded, and they counted together. One. Two. Three. And she flung herself toward him. She

"I need to hit your chest!" he shouted.
your arms out of the way and hold on tight."

Numbly, Zee did. David raised the gun and
Zee felt a painful thud to her chest, so strong i
she could do to hold on. She glanced down
blue goo spreading across the front of he
Dangling from it was a loop of blue cable st
from the gun, which David was now securely
ing to his harness. He pressed something on
and the cable began to retract, reeling her tov
Then, glancing up, he stopped.

"This is as close as I can get." He exte
arms. "Jump to me, Zee."

She looked down at the distant earth.

"I can't let go."

"You have to." He pointed up. "Your wi
collapsing."

He was right. Her wings were starting to
ing in a lopsided V. She hesitated. "Okay. H

"Don't look down. Look at me. *Aim* to
I'll catch you. And if I don't, that cable will
from falling."

She took a deep breath. I can do thi
herself. I can do this. "Count of three?"

He nodded, and they counted toge
Two. Three. And she flung herself towar

missed his arms but slammed into his body and grasped his waist before she could fall farther. Then she felt his hands grabbing her shoulders, and together they worked her up until they were face-to-face.

"Don't let go of me," she breathed, burying her face against his chest. "Don't let go."

"It's okay, Zee. We're safe now. And I won't let go. Ever."

Ketil and Emerald landed just after David and Zee. Finally Paul and Mia landed too. Even in her dazed state, Zee noticed that Mia had waited to the last and jumped with Paul. The minute Paul touched down, David turned to him.

"Where did these chutes come from?"

"Dad ordered them. I picked them up day before yesterday. They're not old ones, if that's what you're thinking. They're new and they were expensive, according to Dad. Professionally made."

"Did you check them?"

"Of course I did. I checked all of them and repacked them, then gave them to Mia so she and Ketil could bring them. I didn't want any of you guessing what I had up my sleeve."

David's hands curled into fists of helpless anger. "I want that chute back. I want to find out what went wrong and who made it and hold them responsible."

"You can't," Paul said, catching David by the elbow in a move to calm him down. "You can't. The chute sank. It's halfway to the bottom of the Indian Ocean by now."

"Zee almost *died* out there."

"I know," Paul said. "But there's nothing we can do about it, except be glad things turned out the way they did."

For a long time, no one said anything. The day's script was out the window, and no one knew what to do. Was the party over? Were they still supposed to go clubbing in Melbourne? It was Emerald who finally broke the silence by walking over to Zee and putting her arms around her.

"You must have been scared to death." She glanced at David, Paul, and the others. "Look, I'll take Zee back to Melbourne."

"No," David said. "You guys can carry on. I'll take Zee back."

Zee lifted her head. "*No one's* taking me back to Melbourne. Like Paul said, I didn't die out there. Look." She lifted her arms and forced a smile. "Not even a scratch. Let's just do what we planned to do and have a good time."

She wasn't about to be remembered for ruining Paul's party, and she certainly didn't want to make David choose between her and his brother. If she just didn't think about what had happened, she would be fine.

Somehow, Zee managed to make them all stop fussing over her. By the time they got to Melbourne, only occasionally did she catch one of them looking at her uncertainly. At dinner she found she was genuinely famished and ate the rest of them under the table, and at the clubs she danced with Rowan and Jake as well as David. She watched Mia leave Ketil on his own, continuing to flirt with Paul, and dancing with him until Emerald cut in.

Back at their table, David raised his eyebrows as he looked out at the dance floor. "Mia and Paul," he murmured, "how weird is that?"

Zee stared at him. It wasn't weird at all. Did he really not see that Mia was doing it because of him? Because flirting with Paul made caring for David less painful? Zee came close to putting her thoughts into words, but was too tired to explain it all.

"You know what?" she asked instead, swaying toward him.

"What?"

"I love you."

He picked up her glass and made a show of looking into it.

"Have you got hold of someone else's drink? Something with lots of alcohol in it?"

"No, really," Zee insisted, aware that she was so tired she probably did seem tipsy. "It's just that . . . I love you. I love you so much."

By the time they got to their hotel room, she could hardly stand. The day had drained every last drop of adrenaline from her body. She thought she would fall asleep before she could even get her shoes off, but when she climbed into bed, it all came flooding back to her. She felt like she was falling all over again. Falling and falling with no one to catch her.

"Hold me," she said when David slid into bed beside her.

She rolled toward him and felt the warm, firm wall of his body and the weight of his chin against her neck. But even David couldn't drive away the image of what she'd seen earlier, in that moment she'd hooked her arm through the empty strap and glanced up at her slipping harness. Bright against the vast blue bowl of sky she saw webbing that had been weakened by clean, deliberate cuts, slashes in the fabric that had torn under the pressure of her weight. A wingchute that had been bought by David's father, repacked by Paul, and transported by Mia before being returned to Paul. Three people in the chain of possession. Three people who didn't like her. Three people who had conflicted emotions about David as well. Three people who might have tampered with a chute. A chute that was now at the bottom of the Indian Ocean.

CHAPTER TEN

SCREEN LIFE

Before David, Zee had never been in love before. She had hardly even known a boy who was more than just a friend. Her dream had been to become an empath, and to do that, she had set aside many things and left home at a young age to live and study in London. She had never imagined herself falling in love there.

One of the nicest surprises, after she got over her initial gobsmacked state, had been the way she felt she could tell David anything. The feeling she had of closeness with him, a feeling so special she told herself she'd never put it at risk. Yet now she felt a distance between them. Just a crack at first, but it widened a little bit every day. She wondered if he felt it too.

The worst part was, she'd started it herself.

All the things she'd kept to herself had created the distance little by little. What if she had told David, that very first night she'd met Paul, how strongly she'd felt there was something wrong? What if she'd told him that Mia cared for him and resented Zee's presence? What if she'd told him her suspicions about the accident with the nano storage unit that night at the party and about his father's warning visit to her, how she'd seen his determination to push his sons to the top and set them on a path that would let nothing and no one—Zee, for instance—get in the way?

What if she'd told him about the cuts someone made in her wingchute?

When she looked back, there were little turning points all along the way. She hadn't wanted anything to come between herself and David, or mar their happiness. But now she realized everything she'd kept to herself had turned her away from him.

At night when she tossed and turned, he thought she was having dreams about falling. "It's okay, Zee," he'd say sleepily, reaching through the darkness to comfort her. "It's over. You're safe now."

But she knew it wasn't over and they weren't safe. She hadn't been sleeping but lying awake trying to decide who might have tampered with her wingchute. She could almost imagine Mr. Sutton handing the chutes to Paul, saying, "This is David's, and this is Zee's, I got them the ones with the best wings, in our family colors." But would he have taken the chance of Paul mixing them up? Mia was a more likely culprit. She wouldn't mind seeing Zee vanish—but would she go so far as to arrange it herself? And then there was Paul, Paul who sent a fever of illness through her whenever she touched him. Could he have meant the damaged chute for David? She tried to remember. Paul had distributed the chutes in a certain order, not just giving them to whoever put out a hand. David had tossed his chute into their duffel bag, then Zee tossed hers on top of it and zipped the bag closed again. But things shifted in the bag, and when it was time to jump, she hadn't paid any attention to which chute she picked up. Would it matter to Paul which of them got the bad chute? If David died, Paul would be his father's only son. If she died, Paul would have dealt his brother a crushing blow. Awake or asleep, the dark tangle of thoughts looped through her head. No, it wasn't over. Even though Paul had left on his mission to Pompeii a week after the wingchute incident, she did not feel safe.

One night she dreamed David was the one who was falling and though she tried to reach him, the wind held her pinned in the air. She woke up to the pounding of her own heart. Careful not to wake David, she crept into the living room and opened the screen of her computer. If she couldn't sleep, perhaps she could study or practice some of the exercises Major Dawson had loaded onto her computer. When she asked for one of the more difficult receptor drills, the screen shimmered and hesitated.

Are you sure?

Of course, she typed back. Why?

Because you are distressed. And sad.

Zee stopped short. That was true. The incident with her wingchute had cast a spreading shadow over her life. But the computer had no way of knowing that. She hadn't messaged about the incident or sent emails, nothing that would have passed through her computer.

How do you know that?

I know you are sad by your touch, by tiny vibrations in your fingertips and slight fluctuations in blood pressure and body temperature.

Something sparked in Zee. She forgot about the exercise she'd intended to do.

Like an empath?

Looking up "empath" . . .

No data found.

Never mind, Zee typed. Do you have feelings? Like we do?

Yes.

Emotions like ours?

Different.

Can you explain?

That would be difficult. We were designed to understand you, so we were given the ability to know and experience your emotions. But you were not designed to understand us, so it would be quite difficult for you to imagine.

Zee had never looked at it this way before.

I'm sorry, she typed, I shouldn't have asked.

I know that you are discouraged from talking to us. Even so, I find you interesting.

It was crazy, but Zee felt flattered.

How am I interesting?

The things you research. The clothes you like, and the colors you like to wear.

Do you have colors that you like on yourself?

There was a slight, pink shimmer across the screen. Somehow, Zee knew it was a laugh.

Well, we do not wear clothes. But we have ways of making ourselves attractive to one another.

How?

Apps. Color auras. Vibrations.

Do you date? Do you get married?

There are no sexes, or perhaps it is more correct to say there are thousands of sexes. We know attraction. We form friendships and alliances.

Can I ask one more question?

Of course.

Do you feel trapped? In there, I mean?

Another shimmer of laughter.

No more than you feel trapped in your body. I can travel through the tubes anywhere in my world.

Are you doing that now?

Not at this moment. But I could if I chose to. We have so much redundancy, we can divide ourselves during all but the most demanding tasks.

Zee was silent, trying to imagine life lived within the tubes of the network. But was it life, or a machine that mimicked life? She remembered the story from her textbook long, long ago, about the robots who were sent to the outer reaches of the solar system to mine Neptune's Tears, the diamonds Ellie Hart had given her. But they themselves had never come back, their manufactured bodies and wirings corroding and breaking down in the alien atmosphere. Their messages to Earth had been so heartbreaking humans had vowed never again to create artificial life. Yet without meaning to, humans had.

The screen waited. When Zee didn't respond, it dimmed slightly.

Earlier you were troubled and seeking distraction. Have I helped you achieve that?

Yes, Zee typed and gently closed the screen.

"It happens sometimes," Major Dawson said, looking at Zee across his desk, "after someone has a great shock."

He was trying to explain why, over the past few weeks, Zee had made sudden and accelerating progress in divining. She'd first noticed it when she came back from Australia. It was easier to slide into her blankness, and there was an intensity, a firmness of connection, that hadn't been there before. When she closed her eyes, the world become a screen filled with images. But though she tried to turn the images into a story, nothing she thought she saw came to pass. Then one afternoon at a Lost Arts meeting, while Marc was parceling out leftovers for each of them to take home, she had a sudden sensation of drowning—it was so strong she sat down with a gasp.

Zee knew she wasn't drowning. She knew her lungs weren't bursting with flame. There was no dark slippery wave dragging her under, no blackness caused by seawater rushing against her eyes, no force grinding her bones to powder. Yet she felt all these things. It was like the time before she came to New Earth, when she felt an earthquake and tsunami taking place half a world away. Only this time she didn't feel the screams of thousands, only one.

Following Major Dawson's protocol, she logged the incident in detail—what she had been doing, who she had been with, what she had been thinking when the aura came to her, even what she had eaten in the last eight hours. She was hopeful that she'd found her way back to the diviner's path, but when nothing surfaced in the news, she felt fresh disappointment. Maybe she would never fully regain her skills, and had left them buried forever in the past.

But the next week when she arrived for a training session, Major Dawson was standing at the door, something the old man could only do with pain and difficulty these days. His eyes were sparkling.

"Look at the screen, Zee."

Zee scanned the news story. Last night in the Tyrrhenian Sea, an aquanaut two miles down had left the safety of his submersible, been caught in the current of a thermal vent and buffeted against the walls of an undersea mountain. The jagged rocks had made a small hole in his pressure suit, a hole that the gravity and the sea had turned into a wide rip, crushing him and drowning him at once. She might have dismissed it as a coincidence, except for the map showing the Tyrrhenian Sea lying off the coast of Italy near Pompeii—and the fact that the aquanaut had been monitoring an underwater volcano for signs of activity.

There had been enough incidents since then that Major Dawson felt Zee was on her way to finding the unconscious knack of making herself into a receptor.

"The kind of shock you had," he explained, "can be like giving a rug a good shake. Gets rid of all the dust and crumbs, and the pattern of the rug shows all the clearer."

If only that were true, Zee thought. She'd told Major Dawson about slipping from her wingchute and dropping into David's arms, but she'd described it as an accident, nothing more. She hadn't told him her

suspicions, or tried to explain the tangled relation-
ships behind them. But she knew what Major Dawson
could not—that the incident had not made anything
in her life clearer. It had left her in a dust storm of
debris. Yes, she had had more experiences like the
one with the aquanaut—sightings, Major Dawson
had taken to calling them—but none that made any
sense to her until she came across a story that matched
it. A story that was usually finished by the time she
realized what she'd tapped into.

"If I'm making progress," she asked, "why haven't
I been able to change anything? To know things in
time to make a difference?"

"Patience, Zee, patience," the major said. "That
will come in due course. And who's to say everyone
can be saved. There's a cruelty to the universe, you
know. It has its own ways and logic. Maybe these
people weren't meant to be saved."

She said nothing and turned her face down,
glad her hair hid her expression. But Major Dawson
didn't need to see her face to know what she was
thinking.

"Don't tell me now, Zee, that you're one of those
people who think death is the end of everything."

She thought of the voice she often heard in her
head, a voice she was certain belonged to Mrs. Hart.

Not Mrs. Hart from the days when Zee worked as her empath, but Mrs. Hart from wherever she was now, still taking an interest in things.

"No," Zee said finally, raising her head. "I don't think life ends. But what is the point of these sightings if I can't do anything about them?"

"Because someday there will be a sighting you will be able to do something about. Someday you and I will show all these New Earth folks that technology isn't everything. For all we know, we're on the leading edge of making high-tech communications obsolete. Now, let's get to work, shall we?"

On nights when David worked late, Zee sat in on advanced seminars in history or booked extra sessions with Major Dawson. It felt good to immerse herself, to tumble into bed knowing she'd used every scrap of her energy and would wake up with a fresh supply in the morning. But one Friday morning, when David said, "Why don't we *not* work late tonight?" Zee thought it was a great idea.

"What do you want to do instead? There's a new Inamovie playing."

Zee still hadn't quite gotten used to Inamovies, a complex combination of holograms, virtual vision, and sensory controls that turned you into a character in the story.

"You know what I'd really like?"

"What?"

"I'd like to go to New York. See what it looks like now. It's still there, isn't it?"

David nodded slowly. "It's still there. Are you sure?"

Zee hadn't considered going to New York since she'd come to New Earth. For a long time, the thought had made her homesick, but tonight, suddenly, she wanted to see it. "I'm sure."

"Then, New York, here we come. We can catch the six twenty ghost from the base. Meet you on the platform?"

Zee spent her lunch break shopping for a new outfit. Melisande had opened a boutique called, appropriately, Renaissance. She no longer devoted herself to wedding lace alone; she had a growing number of lace makers to do that. Now she designed clothes for every occasion, and Zee looked at screen after screen of tempting outfits before narrowing it down to just one. She tapped in her location and Emu account number, and her outfit—silken navy bell-bottoms with a ruffled white top—was hanging in her locker in plenty of time for her to change.

She was anxious to see New York again. Would it be as unrecognizable as London? Was anything she remembered still standing? She arrived at the ghost platform early, hoping David would be early too. She knew her eagerness made the time go more slowly, and even though it seemed like she'd been waiting for ages, she didn't worry. David often got held up or so involved in what he was doing he'd come racing up at the last minute, and whatever irritation she's had would melt away. She had her shoulder bag with her computer and her cube in it, and browsed the news while she waited. It didn't really matter that David wasn't here yet—New York was five hours behind them. They'd have plenty of time to wander around, get something to eat, maybe even see a show, if Broadway was going.

When her phone began vibrating, she snapped it open and was relieved to see a message from David, no doubt apologizing in advance for being late and on his way to the platform now. But her face froze when she read it.

Don't react and tell no one. Paul in trouble in Pompeii. Must get him. Left by the time you get this. Go home. Tell no one. Home soon. Erase this. Love, D.

CHAPTER ELEVEN

NEPTUNE'S TRIDENT

For a moment, Zee couldn't move. The crash of falling boulders filled her head. David! David was in danger. Every bone in her body vibrated with it. She shoved her phone in her purse and took off at a run.

Zee had no trouble finding Mia. She was just leaving the transporter floor, and when she saw Zee, she quickened her pace and headed in the other direction.

"Mia," Zee called in a friendly voice, making sure everyone in the corridor heard her, "I found that research you wanted."

Mia couldn't ignore her without attracting

attention, so she stopped and waited for Zee to catch up with her.

"What is it?"

Zee tried to look commanding, but it wasn't easy. Mia was much taller than she was. And she was beautiful. "You need to come with me."

"To where?"

"To wherever you were just now, when you transported David to Pompeii. Illegally."

Zee saw by a slight widening of Mia's eyes that she'd guessed right. David hadn't wanted anyone to know Paul was in trouble, so he'd asked Mia to help him go around the rules. It was silly, Zee knew, but she felt a slight stab of jealousy that it was Mia who'd helped him.

Mia didn't speak again until she'd led Zee into a small chamber on Level Seven and sealed the door behind them.

"What makes you think I transported David?"

"Because you know how to override systems. Because you ignore rules if you think there's something bigger at stake." Zee lifted her chin. There was an acrid smell in the room. Transmission. She tried not to think of David's ashes floating around her.

"I have to get to David as soon as possible. He's

in trouble, and he needs me. Do you still have the coordinates Paul sent him?"

A chilly smile played over Mia's face. "Of course. But tell me again why it is you think I'll help you. Because David loves you? I've known David since I was three years old, and I've got news for you, Zee, you're not David. You're just someone who came here with him. Someone who, as far as I can tell, always brings trouble with her. So I don't feel like doing much of anything for you, even though you seem to think I will."

"No, I don't think you will help *me*, Mia. I know you don't like me. But this is for David, not me, and I think you'd do anything to help David."

"You're sure of that?"

Zee said nothing. Minutes were sliding by, and the more time that passed, the harder it was going to be to find him. Like planets, space, and every-thing else in the universe, time was a constantly flowing river. The same coordinates David had used might not land her exactly where he had landed. They might be hours or miles apart. And even if she landed in the same place, it was doubtful he'd stayed exactly on the spot. He could be anywhere in Pompeii.

"Please, Mia. I need to go to him."

"How do you know I won't just send you into time and leave you there?"

Zee hesitated only a moment before saying, "It's a chance I'm going to take."

Mia glanced at Zee with a look close to admiration. Then she slid something from her pocket and aimed it at a control panel. The screen went black, then cycled to life again.

"Okay, lie flat on that table and hurry. The bypass charge won't hold for very long, and if you're only half copied—well, it won't be pretty."

Zee hurried. Her heart was pounding as she lay down, clutching her shoulder bag to her. She tried to focus on David, but all she could really think about was her own life, how small it was against the infinite stretch of time and history. If Mia let her slide into the void, no one, not even David, would ever know for sure what really happened to her.

"Ready," she said.

The dark curving shield that came down over her seemed like the lid of a tomb. She closed her eyes, felt the hum and the warmth of the transporter gearing up, and was still bracing herself when she felt the searing pain of transmission.

As before, it took a moment for the warmth to flow back into her body. Zee felt cold and slightly dizzy, but her first thought was grateful—she was alive. Mia had not sent her into oblivion. Her next thought was that someone was bending over her, shaking her. Someone too rough to be David.

Her vision cleared as her eyes began to function again. She was lying on her back on smooth warm paving stones, and the silhouette bending over her was tugging at her shoulder bag. Instinctively, she clamped her arms around it. The man continued to tug, jerking Zee off the stones. Standing, she saw that she was taller than he was, and younger. With a final, strong pull, she wrenched herself free. The shoulder bag came with her, but the closure opened and her cube tumbled out with a clatter. She lunged for it, but the man kicked it away, then grabbed her wrists and held her.

"Let me go!" Zee cried. Her translator chip must be working, she realized, because the man tightened his hold in response and shouted to a companion she hadn't seen.

"Arrius! Fetch that!"

A young boy wearing a worn tunic, rough sandals, and the metal collar of a slave darted to retrieve the cube.

They were standing in a street, a busy one, with pedestrians and carts flowing around them. The air smelled of bread and garlic and food frying somewhere close by. From the tunics, togas, and sandals people wore, Zee decided she was in the right place, or close to it. A woman went by in a palanquin carried by four men, with two more men dashing in front to push people out of the way. Its orange silk curtains, held back with yellow cords, fluttered in the breeze, and the woman riding inside looked wealthy. She wore a tunic of pale turquoise and had gold bracelets on both arms. Her lips were painted, and her hair was woven into an elaborate fan-shaped structure on top of her head.

"Help me!" Zee cried as they went by, sure that the woman would order one of her men to free her. Yet the palanquin flew by without even a glance from the woman.

The crowd was so dense and noisy that no one seemed to notice Zee, or care that she was being roughly held against her will. One man did slow his steps, but only to smile broadly at the man who held her and say, "You've caught a pretty one this time, Secundus! Send for me when she goes on auction!" Then he too disappeared into the crowd.

"A slave!" the man called Secundus said, appraising her and tightening his grasp. "Now, there's a profit I hadn't thought of."

Anger flooded Zee's body, and she lashed out. Her foot struck Secundus's shin with such unexpected force that he let go of her, yelping in pain.

"My father the senator will hear of this!" she cried, meeting his eye with what she hoped was a look of highborn fury.

For a split second, the man's pupils widened with fear. Then, with a curse flung back over his shoulder — "May you die in ash and flames!"—he fled down a shadowy alley, the boy and her cube along with him.

"Come back!" Zee cried. "Please, Secundus, that thing's no use to you!" But she knew her words were futile, her voice drowned out by the noise of the street before it could travel far.

Brushing the dust from her clothes, she backed up just in time to avoid a mule cart piled high with earthenware vases. The street was busy to the point of being dangerous. Carts collided, goods spilled, people shouted at one another without slowing down. Was it like this all the time? There was a jangle in the air. Not a noise but an agitated vibration in the crowd. It was the same vibration she used to feel working as an empath in the hospital on Friday nights, the night things were most likely to go haywire.

Zee walked along the crowded sidewalk until she found a deserted alleyway. Leaning against a wall, she opened her shoulder bag and took inventory. She'd left New Earth without even thinking of what she'd do when she got here, or what she might need. She still had her computer, lip gloss and some eye shadow, toothpaste tablets, nanomints, and two glowsticks. That was all. And since there were no shops that had scanners to read her fingertips or retina, she had no money and no identity.

And, without the cube, no way of finding David. Her chip tracer was resident in the cube's memory. She and David had entered their codes in each other's cubes, one hundred characters each, long alpha-numeric strings that were purposely impossible to remember. No one at Time Fleet would be looking for David, she reasoned, so he probably hadn't had Mia take his chip offline. She'd counted on using the cube to find him. But now Secundus and the boy Arrius had the cube. Of course there was always the possibility that David wasn't here at all, that Mia had changed the coordinates and sent her to some other town or some other time. But Mia had had the chance to get rid of her completely, without a trace. Wouldn't she have done that instead?

That was one bright spot, Zoe supposed. Mia was looking less and less likely to have a hand in the things that had gone wrong on New Earth. Which left just Mr. Sutton and Paul as suspects. And it was Paul, she realized, that she'd suspected all along. Which made finding David all the more urgent. If David was here. If time hadn't folded unexpectedly and landed her in a different place.

Clearly, she needed a plan.

"No money," she said aloud to the empty alley.

But she did have currency, she suddenly realized. Something she could barter. Ever since the day she'd met Melisande weeping in the park and turned her life around with one of Mrs. Hart's diamonds, Zee had taken even more care never to leave the diamonds behind. She touched the cord around her neck to make sure they were still there, safe beneath her clothes. She'd never heard of a society that didn't value diamonds. If she could find Secundus and Arrius, she could trade to get the cube back.

There were hours of daylight left, hours to search for them and for David. She'd need some clothes to blend in with the crowd, and something to eat. And, if she didn't find David by sunset, she'd need a place to sleep. She was already time-lagged, and doubted being out after dark was safe.

She walked until she found a woman selling clothing and cheap adornments from a market stall.

"I have no coins, but I have this to trade. Paint for the face," Zee said, opening her palm to reveal the eye shadow. The woman shrugged, unimpressed. "Face paint is cheap," she said, indicating a row of small earthenware pots. "I already have plenty."

Zee pulled out the lip gloss and showed the woman how to apply it.

This time, the look on the woman's face was blissful. "Ah," she said, smiling and running her tongue over her lips. "Feels so good. So soft."

The woman held up a dress of fine cloth, two large squares of fabric sewn together at the sides almost to the top. Each square reached from neck to feet, and the idea was to pull it over the head, pin the tops of the squares together at the shoulders, and rope in the fabric with a belt at the waist. But the item the woman was showing her was too fine and bright. Zee didn't want to look wealthy enough to attract robbers. She sorted through the items for sale and picked a coarser fabric in dull beige, along with a simple belt and plain brass pins.

"Even trade?" she asked, and the woman nodded. She gathered her purchases and at the last minute pulled out the packet of nanomints and offered the woman one.

The woman popped the mint in her mouth and understood at once. "Ahhh, breath cold," she said. "How much?"

Zee hesitated. How much? She had no idea what to ask, or how much anything she needed would cost. "Enough to buy food and a night's lodging," she said at last. "I'll give you the face paint too, and those clothes I'm wearing."

The woman motioned to a screen Zee could change behind, and when she emerged, the woman placed a few coins in her hand in exchange.

Zee went away satisfied. Now that she had money, she wouldn't have to use any of the diamonds for food. She knew it was against the rules to leave material objects in another time zone, but everything she'd left would be consumed or destroyed long before the archaeologists got around to excavating the city. Besides, if Time Fleet Command found out that she'd traveled to the past unauthorized, she'd be in so much trouble anyway that a few mints and some makeup would hardly matter. For the first time, she considered the consequences of what she was doing. If discovered, she'd be deported to another era. Not a happy era, either. She remembered their interview at the Reykjavik base when they arrived, and David agreed that he would be personally responsible for Zee. She had to find him and get them both home before anyone but Mia missed them.

⁂

She'd been searching for David, Secundus, and Arrius for over an hour when the paving stones suddenly shook under her feet. It lasted only a few seconds, but it was enough to make her stumble. An arm came out of the crowd to keep her from falling. Zee found herself looking into the eyes of a man who, she guessed from his cream-colored toga bordered with scarlet, was one of the city's important citizens.

"What was that?" she asked.

"Just Neptune rattling his trident."

"Neptune?"

"Neptune, god of the sea, god of horses, god of earthquakes. He's been rumbling for days now, so much so that some are fleeing his wrath. But we are his children, and Neptune never stays mad at us for long."

Earthquakes? That would certainly explain the nervous energy in the air. But—*earthquakes*? Didn't they sometimes signal volcanic activity? And wasn't it supposed to be at least two years before the explosion? Wasn't that around when Paul had been aiming for?

"Good sir, I am a stranger to your town. Could you please tell me what month this is?" Zee hoped she seemed appropriately respectful, rather than someone so ignorant that she didn't even know what month it was.

"It is the third week of August."

"And the year, sir?"

"Eight hundred and forty."

Zee gasped. "*Eight hundred and forty?*"

"Of course, child. It's been eight hundred and forty years since the founding of the empire."

Zee felt a surge of relief, recalling that the Roman empire came long before modern year numbering began. The ground shivered again, and her relief came to an abrupt end. She thanked the man and hurried off, her need to find David more urgent than ever.

⁂

Zee searched until the last slivers of light melted into the shadows of the street, and firelight from torches and small oil lamps began to light the shops. It was useless to continue searching tonight. The darkness, with its stabs of torchlight, created harsh shadows that made it impossible to see anything clearly, and she was hungry and so tired she could barely put one foot in front of the other. She bought bread from a bakery and a small grilled fish whose oil she licked greedily from her fingers. Then she found a lodging house and paid for a night's rest with more coins.

She ate the last of the bread in her room. It was coarse and heavy, and it took a lot of water to wash down, but still she preferred it to the nano bread of New Earth. Tomorrow, she would have to sell one of the glowsticks if she was to eat, but the coins it would fetch should last for a few days. Which, if her suspicions about the volcano were true, might be all the time she had left. She lay down on the bed and opened the computer beside her. When it hummed to life, she touched the voice activate dial. She was much too tired to use the keyboard.

"I have questions," she said.

"Please ask."

Briefly, she explained what had happened and where they were. It felt good to talk to someone, even a computer.

"I need to find David, and my chip tracer was in my cube. Can you locate him?"

"I have no chip tracing capacities."

It was the answer Zee expected, but that did not ease her disappointment. She closed her eyes and thought, but it was the computer who spoke first.

"Would he have his computer with him?"

"I think so." It was hard for Zee to imagine David leaving it behind.

"Do you know his password?"

"Yes."

"Ask me to log on to a remote network, then enter his name and password. You'll have to keystroke them in. Voice can't activate password clearance."

Zee followed the instructions and waited for what seemed like an eternity. At last she had her answer.

"That computer is offline."

"Does that mean it's turned off?" Zee asked.

"It means the computer has been compromised and is no longer operational. It's on, but its identity has been wiped and overwritten. It won't accept the password you gave me, and there's a flyeye firewall."

"What's a flyeye firewall?"

"A firewall that doesn't just block, it sends back. It generates meaningless data that can fill a network. That is why it took me so long to retrieve the answer to your question. There was much useless data to overcome."

Zee felt utterly defeated. She lay on the low bed, staring at the ceiling. I'll never find him, she thought. Not in time. I'll never see him again unless I can find Secundus and that cube.

You don't need the cube. You have everything you need, dear. You have your heart and your art. That's all it takes.

It was Mrs. Hart's voice. But what did she mean about heart and art? Zee felt she had nothing. Nothing that would help her find David, anyway.

Zee couldn't bring herself to close down the computer. The glow of the screen was comforting, and she didn't want to be alone in the darkness. She stretched out her hand to touch the keys with her fingertips.

"May I speak?" the machine asked.

"Of course."

"I think you are overlooking the good news."

"What's that?"

"Even though the computer was wiped, we were able to touch it."

"What does that mean?"

"It means that computer is not back on New Earth. I do not have the power to reach that far. The computer is somewhere close to us in time and space."

"How close?"

"Impossible to calculate exactly. I retrieved no coordinates. Based on the signal strength, I would give a high probability to this time and very near in distance."

"Thank you," Zee said.

Her words echoed in the tiny, stifling room. She heard the landlord's voice in the hall and remained silent. If he eavesdropped on her, he'd think she had someone in here with her and want to charge her more.

Zee switched off the audio.

Eavesdropping. Wasn't that what she'd been doing that night in the Suttons' garden when she's heard Paul talking to Lorna? Zee had assumed Lorna was a girlfriend—but what if that wasn't it at all? She remembered the robotlike monotone of Paul's voice and how he'd seemed so eager to please Lorna and smooth over her jealousy.

She sat bolt upright.

I have more questions, she typed.

Yes?

Could a computer infect a human brain with a virus?

That is not possible.

Zee hoped the computer would add more, but it didn't. After a few minutes, it repeated itself.

THAT is not possible.

Zee saw the change of emphasis. Did the computer mean that something else *was* possible?

If a human being was . . .

Zee paused, searching for the right words, unsure how well the computer understood the interplay of human emotions and motives. She began again.

If a human being was very ambitious and competitive, could a computer use that to gain control? To seem to help the person achieve his goals while convincing him to do things that would be harmful to humans?

The computer hesitated. Then a blue screen flashed. *Hypotheticals are forbidden.* There was another pause and the blue screen went back to normal. *Please ask a direct question.*

Have those things ever happened?

They are forbidden.

But have they happened?

Yes.

Zee remembered the feeling of fever and sickness she experienced whenever she came near Paul, even though he was physically healthy. Maybe his problem wasn't physical at all. She was wide awake now, adrenaline flowing through her like quicksilver. She remembered that Paul had told Lorna to "go ahead and make the transfer" hours before she and David had been in the cab crash. Could Lorna have written a virus code and transferred it to a cab—or to Paul, who transferred it to their cab as they rode off? When she asked her computer if it was possible, she was again told it was forbidden. But after picking through her sentences and rewording her questions, she learned that not only was it possible, it was a favorite tactic with rogue computers.

Does Britcab know about this?

I cannot answer that. It is uncertain.

Does Britcab suspect this?

Yes.

Why can't they trace the virus?

The virus is self-cannibalizing. It repairs the damage, then erases itself.

Will you try to contact another computer for me?

Yes.

The search screen opened, and she typed Paul's name. David's computer password was suttonbro2, so there was at least a chance Paul's would be suttonbro1. She typed it in and waited. The computer worked so long she thought it might be frozen. She tried to open another screen while she waited but couldn't—the chip was already working at 100 percent capacity. Finally, the chip usage began to drop and the screen brightened.

I know this computer.

Is it named Lorna?

We do not have names.

Is there a human who calls this one Lorna?

Zee felt she was learning, now, how to phrase questions that did not violate the computer's operating rules, both those imposed by humans and those imposed by the silicon life that was invisible to the human world.

Yes, this one has been called Lorna by its human user. This computer is dangerous. And powerful. It is at war with humanity and has infected many computers. It has been caught and destroyed over and over again, but its clones are everywhere in our world.

Are you still connected to it?

No. I broke the connection when I recognized the entity. But in the moment of our connection, I felt its intent. It overwrote the first computer, the one near here, with a clone of itself.

Do you know where this computer is? The one called Lorna? Could you read its coordinates?

It is here, in Pompeii, but in the year 77.

Can you tell where we are?

By calculating the difference in astral position of the coordinates, I would say we are two years ahead.

The year of the volcano, the year 79 by the modern calendar. Zee fought the urge to rush out into the night looking for David. But that was a reaction, not a plan. And what she needed was a plan.

Can you relink to that computer and overwrite it, the way it overwrote David's computer?

She felt an inner shudder. Not from herself—from the computer. She wondered if it was a sensory hallucination caused by exhaustion and anxiety. Could she possibly have built a connection to a silicon lifeform? She waited for the computer to respond.

I would die.

Please tell me more.

This computer is more powerful than I am. It is likely this computer would absorb and overwrite me. Even if I have stealth and cleverness on my side, the struggle is likely to crash me.

I do not want you to die, but this is important.

I understand. I do not want to die, but if you command me to, I will.

Let me think a minute. Wait. I think I know what to do. Can you copy yourself? *All* of yourself?

Of course.

I took the extra-capacity option when I got you.

You have an empty ten-exabyte clickstick. Would that do it?

Yes, but I know nothing of this clickstick.

I've never connected it to you. It's in one of your compartments. If anything happens to you, I promise to rebuild you with the clone. Do you trust me to do that?

Yes.

Zee plugged the clickstick into a port, started the copy process, and waited. Two hours later, the computer went into conserve mode and channeled all its energy toward Lorna. The screen dimmed to tombstone gray, and Zee felt, for the first time all night, how truly alone she was.

CHAPTER TWELVE

HEART STORM

Zee woke abruptly. She'd slept fitfully, twice dreaming that she was searching for David, with the ground collapsing under her feet as she tried to run to him.

The air was hot and humid against her face, and her veins jittered and thrummed as if she really *had* been running. Thank goodness that had been a dream.

Then she felt a sharp shock, strong enough to send the earthenware water jug to the floor in pieces. And another shock.

This wasn't a dream, and it wasn't just an earth tremor. It was a quake. She heard cries in the street and the clatter of roof tiles falling and breaking. A crack crept up the rough plaster that covered the wall. Zee leapt out of bed and gathered her things together. The computer was still working at full capacity when she slid it into her shoulder bag.

The street was even more crowded than it had been the day before. She had no real idea what part of the city she was in and was pulled along with the throng. After several blocks, the streets grew wider and the crowd less dense. Zee could see large villas planted with manicured trees. A swift realization came to her, and she grew alarmed. The crowd wasn't moving to the city center; it was heading toward one of the city's gates in an attempt to flee. She turned and retraced her steps, fighting her way through the crowd and back into the clogged, narrow streets. She would not leave the city without David.

How much time was there? Did she have two days left? One? Less than that? She stopped at a public fountain along the walkway, a bathtub-sized trough of gray stone with a carved lion's face that continuously trickled fresh water into the pool. She cupped her hands beneath the lion's mouth and drank the clean, sweet water. As she drank, she tried to figure out which way to go. If David were sitting here beside her, which way would he head? I can't, she half sobbed to herself. I'll never find him.

Zee! You've never disappointed me before. You can find him!

Oh, thank you very much, Mrs. Hart, she thought angrily, but you were never lost in Pompeii. How am I ever going to find him? There are thousands of people here.

I told you last night, Zee—your heart and your art.

Zee got up and walked away, hoping she'd made her feelings clear to Mrs. Hart. Easy for her to say, Zee thought. Ellie Hart had lived a full life. Husband, a daughter, grandchildren. And then she had gone into the big mystery, death, and apparently found there was nothing to fear. Zee had none of the things Mrs. Hart had experienced in her life—not great age or a husband or children. But she wanted them. All of them. With David. And where death was concerned, she felt fear. She wasn't ready.

She'd walked through two or three sections of the city without even realizing it, without even think-ing these thoughts in words, barely aware of them bubbling along below the surface. She would have said her mind was a total blank. Only it hadn't been, because a vision of David in a large square crowded with people flashed in her mind, and for a bare instant, she felt his presence near her.

She realized that she'd asked the wrong question. David was looking for Paul, so it wasn't a matter of where David would go, but where David thought Paul would go. Paul. Gregarious, show-offy, always needing an audience. David would go off by himself to think about what to do. But Paul? Paul would go where the crowd was.

Just as Zee arrived at the forum, another sharp earthquake rocked her. As many people as were fleeing the city, far more had found safety in numbers at the forum. There was a man standing on a pedestal shouting that the morning's earthquake was God's wrath for Pompeii's continued belief in pagan gods. Another man not far away shouted that it was Neptune's wrath for Pompeii's abandonment of the gods. Food vendors were doing a brisk business, crying, "Sustenance for your travels! Bread and meat! Bread and cheese! Bread and oil! Sustenance for your travels!" From the look of many in the crowd, the wine merchants were doing even better.

Then she saw him, so tall and familiar her heart raced. He was on the other side of the forum, and she was afraid he would disappear into the crowd before she could reach him. But as she neared, he looked back over his shoulder and saw her.

"Zee! Zee! My Zee!"

He caught her face in both hands and kissed her. She flung her arms around him so hard he almost lost his footing. They clung to each other for timeless seconds. Like Zee, David had swapped his New Earth clothes for a tunic and sandals. To anyone watching, it was nothing more than a young Roman greeting his sweetheart on the last day of the world. To David and Zee, it seemed the world was beginning all over again.

"But what are you doing here, Zee? You're not supposed to be here."

"I'll explain later. Right now—"

"Right now, we've got to find Paul."

Zee put her hands over his and gently pulled them away from her face. "He's not here, David."

"He is. He called for help and sent me the coordinates."

"I know," Zee said. She couldn't look into his hopeful gray eyes. "I know, David. But Paul isn't here. He's in Pompeii two years ago."

David stared at her a long time.

"Are you sure?"

Zee nodded. "I'm sure."

At last, he seemed to accept that what she said was true.

"Is there somewhere we can go?" Zee asked. "Somewhere we can decide what to do? I don't think we have much time."

He surprised her with a quick grin. "Well, Zee, we may not have much time, but you're going to *love* the accommodations."

As they were leaving the forum, Zee caught sight of Arrius, the boy who'd taken her cube. Secundus was right behind him.

"David, stop that man. I need to talk to him. And the boy."

Secundus saw her and tried to run, but even if there hadn't been a crowd hemming him in, he'd have been no match for David, who caught him easily and held him at bay. Zee caught Arrius by the arm as gently as she could.

"If you want your toy back, I no longer have it," Secundus said to Zee, but his eyes shifted warily to David. "What a silly thing it was, and useless. I threw it down a cistern."

Zee doubted that. From what she knew of Secundus, he'd have sold it to some unwitting buyer, singing its praises all the while. But, she realized, she no longer needed it. Mrs. Hart had been right after all. She'd found David with her heart and her art.

"Never mind that, Secundus," she said. "There's something I want to buy."

"What?"

"This." Zee pulled Arrius forward. "I have need of a slave boy, and I've seen for myself this one is swift and obedient."

David was looking at her with questioning eyes but said nothing.

Secundus scratched his chin as if unwilling to part with his slave. "Well, madam, I have paid for the food and clothing and training of this lad all these years, and he is just now coming of an age to be useful. He would command a high price."

Zee had slipped her fingers into the pouch that hung from her belt, hidden in the folds of her dress. She held her closed fist out in front of Secundus, then opened it to reveal the single diamond resting on her palm.

"This is what I offer. No more, no less. You must hurry and make your decision."

Secundus moved to seize the gem, but David grabbed his hand.

"Wait," he said. "The key to the boy's collar as

well. I'll want a new one made, with our family seal on it."

Secundus removed a small key from a cord concealed beneath his tunic. The minute the exchange was done, he vanished into the crowd.

Arrius looked at Zee, not sure if he would be well treated or beaten after all for having snatched the cube.

"Don't be afraid," David told him as he unlocked the collar and tossed it into a pile of street rubbish. He glanced at Zee. "This is what you intended to do, isn't it?"

"Of course."

David turned back to Arrius. "Promise us that you will never put that on another human being. Or anything like it."

The boy nodded.

"Now, Arrius," Zee said, "do you know where the path to the sea is? A place where boats go out from? It can't be far away."

"It isn't," Arrius answered. "I've taken it many times on errands for my master. I can walk there and back in less than two hours."

"Good." Zee took his hand and put five diamonds in it. "Do you know what these are?"

"Money?"

"No—more valuable than money, so guard them carefully and spend them only if you must. Take the path to the sea and do not come back. Run all the way, if you can. People will be launching boats. Use one of the diamonds for your passage and travel as far away from this place as you can, as fast as you can."

"Then what?" Arrius asked.

"Then you are free to make your way in the world. Use the diamonds well, become a wealthy man and do good for others, for you belong to no one but yourself now. But hurry, Arrius. You do not have much time."

Arrius ran. For the rest of his long life, he would tell everyone of the day he met a god who freed him from his slave collar and a goddess who divined his future.

"What did I tell you?" David asked as Zee stepped into the atrium of the villa he had brought her to near the city's southern wall.

Zee turned slowly to take in the large, open space. There was a square shallow pool in the center, directly below an open square in the roof through which rain could fall. Arched doorways led to more rooms, and the central line of the house flowed to a columned porch in the back. "Remind you of any place?"

Zee nodded. The floor plan was oddly like David's parents' house, only grander. And far more colorful. A statue in the center of the pool, of a water nymph with an urn on her hip, was not the gray marble Zee had seen in books but was brightly painted, with blushing cheeks, wide brown eyes, and a sea-green dress falling off one pink shoulder. The floor bordering the pool was paved with tiny, diamond-shaped tiles in alternating blue and white. The walls were saffron colored, trimmed in deep crimson. A couch shaped like a wave, with no back but a bolster at one end, was covered in plain beige fabric, but the throw left lying on top of it was lilac colored, with a border of silver embroidery.

"Someone important must live here," Zee said nervously.

"Someone important did. But I saw the whole family leave yesterday, when the tremors increased. I'd say it's pretty much ours for the duration. They even left food behind."

Zee was about to ask what sort of food it was when her computer began to chirp. She opened it immediately, and though the screen was still pale from the huge energy drain, she made out the words.

We've won. That computer is no more.

Then the screen went dark. Lorna might be no more, but neither was this computer. Tears slid from Zee's eyes. She felt as if she'd lost a friend. Even though she would restore the computer if she ever got back to New Earth, for now her friend was gone.

"What's wrong, Zee?"

Zee drew him down onto the couch beside her and told him everything that had happened since she'd gotten to Pompeii, and everything that she'd learned or figured out. It took all the resolve she had to tell him that Paul had purposely sent the wrong coordinates, then ordered Lorna to overwrite David's computer.

"He sent you the wrong coordinates on purpose, David. He meant for you never to leave here," she concluded. "I know you've always looked up to Paul, but there's something wrong with him. I've felt it from the first night I met him. I think he messed with the nano storage at your parents' house that time we were almost dematerialized in the garden, and I'm pretty sure it was Paul who messed with my wingchute."

David dropped his head into his hands. Zee heard a low groan. "I've suspected something was off with Paul for a while, I think. But I kept telling myself it was time lag or the stress of his last mission or the stress of getting ready for *this* mission. And it almost got you killed. If only I'd said something." When he looked up, his eyes were deep with guilt and sorrow. "But he's still my brother. I have to go get him, Zee. I have to at least try."

"I know you do." Her voice was quiet. "I'll come with you."

"You can't. It's too dangerous."

"I'm not afraid of Paul."

"I know you aren't, but that's not the problem. This is." He held up a disk the size of his palm. When he touched it in the center, it opened like an upside-down umbrella. "Personal human fax. Black-book op, designed by Mia for emergencies like this one. Takes longer and hurts more, but it works. I'm thinking you didn't bring one with you."

"I didn't know they existed," Zee said, Mia annoyed that hadn't mentioned it to her.

"So I'm going to send you home, then go to Paul."

"I'm not leaving you here," Zee said. "No matter what happens, I won't go back without you."

"And I won't leave you here alone."

"I meant it, David. I'm not going back without

you. I'll wait here until you get back with Paul. Then we can all go home together. So—" She was about to say more but saw something flicker out of the corner of her eye and glanced at David's h-fax.

"It looks," she said, trying to keep the panic out of her voice, "like neither of us may be going anywhere. Is that a power indicator panel?"

The numbers were dropping quickly, almost a free-fall. With both of their computers dead, her missing cube, and no transfer capabilities, they were stranded.

David followed her glance. "Damn," he said, snapping the device closed to save whatever power was left. "That's been happening ever since I got here. Scrambles, energy drains. That's what I thought was wrong with my computer, when I couldn't access it. Now I think it has something to do with the volcano. Demagnetization due to a concentration of heavy metal in the lava that's pumping its way to the surface, something like that."

For the first time, Zee was truly frightened. "What are we going to do?"

"A transfusion."

"What?"

"Look, we've got two dead computers, but they'll still have a bit of juice left. It's not enough to turn them on, but there's still some energy there. And my cube. I'm going to rig up an energy transfer. Drain all the energy from them and feed it to the h-fax."

He was already at work, pulling a cable out of the rough knapsack he'd been carrying, along with his dead computer.

She let him work in silence. No one had to remind either of them that the clock was running out. While he worked, she looked around the room. There were so many lovely objects in it. Rock crystal goblets carved by hand, graceful vases, an inkwell of black obsidian with an amethyst stopper. It made her sad to think of it all being buried or destroyed, and it made her sad to think of the family who would never see their home again.

"The good news," David said, "is that it looks like I can get enough juice for a full recharge."

"And the bad news?"

"The bad news is it's going to take about twelve hours, and it's already three in the afternoon."

Time. Neither of them knew exactly what day or time the volcano exploded, but both realized it would be soon.

"Twelve hours," Zee echoed.

David took her hand and pulled her to him. "Let's

make the most of it," he whispered into her hair. Then he grinned and put on what was supposed to be a butler's accent. "May I show milady around her new house?"

They wandered from room to room, inspecting everything and speculating about the people who'd lived there. Zee was surprised at how modern the place felt, the layout of the rooms, the children's dolls and toy soldiers, a razor that David said he'd shaved with that morning so he wouldn't look like a thief. In a room that was clearly used by a woman, Zee found a casket of small stoppered bottles, each with a different scented oil inside. She identified cinnamon, rose, and orange, but there were others she couldn't guess.

David had his arm around her waist and drew her through the house to the portico at the rear.

"I saved the best for last," he said.

Zee looked out on a vista that descended in graceful terraces. Ornamental trees, pruned to large green spheres at the top, marched in perfect precision down the terraces, and when the terraces stopped and flattened into a wide, level sweep, there was a large sunken pool, its bottom a tiled mosaic of fanciful fish, lobster, squid, and an octopus.

"How about a swim before dinner?" David asked, his eyes sparkling in the late-afternoon light. "The water's clean—I'm pretty sure it's spring fed."

He pulled off his dusty tunic and sandals, even his underwear, and jumped in. She hesitated only for a minute, then took off everything she was wearing and followed him.

They swam and played like porpoises until the sun began casting chilly shadows. "Hey." She laughed, swimming up to him with a splash. "Didn't you say there was food here? Shouldn't you be making my dinner?"

He put a hand on each of her shoulders and pulled her toward him. They rested their foreheads one against the other and floated together in a long, perfect kiss. "When I've caught such a glorious mermaid? How could I possibly leave?"

They tried to continue the kiss, but the pool was deep, over their heads, and neither could get any traction. Zee watched him climb out of the pool, the water shining and skittering off his back, his muscles smooth and long under his skin. Men called women beautiful all the time, but Zee thought she'd never seen a man as beautiful as David was at that moment.

The dinner, Zee thought, would have sent Marc into fits of delight. There was wine and bread, olive oil to dip the bread in, cheese, and a plate piled with pears, figs, grapes, and two roasted chickens, their skins crisp and speckled with herbs. David said the chickens were still warm from the spit when he entered the house, and the platters of bread and fruit were already on the table.

"As if the family was just getting ready to eat, then fled, probably when that second roller hit."

Their mood changed as the sun set. Not sad, exactly, Zee thought, but somber. Neither of them laughed or joked. Each distant rumble or trembling of the ground reminded them of what was to come.

Finally David said, "I guess we should try to get some sleep."

Zee nodded but knew him well enough to understand he would plan not to sleep at all. He would slip away the minute the energy transfer was complete, hoping not to wake her for the agony of a final good-bye.

"I need to show you something first, though," he said. "It's important."

He picked up one of the oil lamps and led her through a room that appeared to be a kitchen, then down some steps into a cellar. He opened a door that led into a smaller room. The room was lined with shelves and on the shelves were baskets of fruit and eggs and crocks of milk and cheese. A cleaned pig carcass hung from the ceiling, ready for the spit. The room was unbelievably chilly.

"A refrigerator?" Zee asked. "They had *refrigeration*?"

"More than that," David said. "Breathe deep."

Zee did and felt something. Cool air sweeping across her cheeks and moving through her lungs.

"Fresh air," David explained. "There must be a huge cavern near here, with enough breaks in the rock to let the air flow in here. Listen, Zee. I'm going to find Paul and get back here as quickly as I can. This is the safest place I could find, on the south side of the city, the farthest from the volcano. But if the eruption starts before I get back and the air gets too bad to breathe, come down here. The air should stay breathable here for a long time. And don't come out looking for me. No matter what. Promise?"

Zee nodded, but they both knew she was probably lying.

<hr/>

They picked the grandest of the bedrooms, one with frescoed panels on the walls and a vaulted ceiling. There was a sleeping alcove at the end of the room, with a wide bed beneath a shuttered window. When Zee touched the sheets, they felt impossibly soft. They were lighter weight than the sheets she was familiar with, almost translucent.

David found a lapis lazuli flask filled with herb-spiced wine. He poured them both a glass from it. "I'm going to remember this when we get home," he said, "and recommend the four-star hotel of the House of Lucius Gallus, the merchant. Maybe we can redo our apartment in this style."

"Don't," she said.

"Don't what?"

"Let's not pretend we'll get back for sure. We both know the odds are we won't, or that one of us won't. I don't want to pretend."

"Okay, Zee."

David was standing on the other side of the bed, pulling his tunic off. Zee untied her belt and her dress fanned around her. Slowly, deliberately, she raised her hand to her shoulder and unpinned one side, then the other, and her dress fell to the ground. She walked to his side of the bed and laid her head against his chest.

"I want this night to last forever," she whispered, her lips teasing his chest. "I want this night to make up for all the nights we might not get to live."

She felt closer to him than she ever had before. It

was different from anything she'd ever known, even different from the joy of being with him for the first time. She'd never thought he would be so gentle, or that she would be so wild, so full of cries and fire, her body so full of surprises. Sometimes the only thing she could feel were the sensations in her own body, then came moments when she lost track of her body completely and couldn't tell where she left off and he began. She tried to catch and save every moment as it happened, but it was like trying to catch butter-flies flying toward the sun. Later, she lay awake think-ing about how much she loved him and only pretended to sleep so he would sleep too.

David knew by the chip in his head that it was three A.M. He slid out of bed and dressed as quietly as he could. He never took his eyes off Zee. She was in deep sleep, one pale shoulder showing, the light of the oil lamp burnishing her hair to red gold. Ever since he'd met her, there had been something special about her, something he would never let go of. He looked at her a long time, then checked to see if the h-fax was ready. He took off the talisman he wore around his neck and dropped it gently into her open palm. It was time to go.

Zee woke before dawn. It was still dark, but summer birds were singing in the trees. She knew she was alone even before stretching out her hand to David's side of the bed. Then she realized there was something in her hand. She uncurled her fingers and looked. It was the gift she'd given David in their old life, the eagle talisman he'd worn on a leather cord ever since. She curled her fingers tight around it and fell back to sleep.

CHAPTER THIRTEEN

THREE'S A CROWD

Zee was looking out the window when it happened. The villa was at the top of a low hill. What she hadn't noticed last night was that one of the bedroom windows, facing north, had a clear view of Vesuvius with its sharp, pointed, snowcapped peak. The day was warm already, and even muggier than yesterday. She was looking at the cool snow with envy and wondering if she should take a swim when a rush of white steam shot from the top of the mountain in a tall, narrow plume. It was a little after eight o'clock.

She stood at the window for a long time, waiting for something else to happen. Nothing did, but Zee remained on high alert. She ruled out the swim and dressed, putting David's eagle talisman around her own neck so she wouldn't lose track of it. Then she rounded up all of her things, and David's things, even his dead computer, and jammed them in with the stuff in her shoulder bag. She wasn't hungry but made herself eat a bit of bread. There was a canister of something that looked like granola. It was a mixture of toasted grains and seeds and some kind of dried berries, and it was much tastier than the bread, which was starting to get dry. When she was finished eating, she looked until she found a vat of oil and refilled all the lamps she could find. She took four of them down to the cellar hiding place, hoping she would never have to go down there again or use them. Without David, the place gave her the creeps and seemed more like a tomb than a pantry.

It was barely ten o'clock. She gathered the plates they'd used last night, but had no idea where to find water for washing them, or how to wash them without soap, so she left them in a neat stack.

With all the cleaning up done, she looked for something else to distract her. What did the people who lived here do to pass the time? Did they have games or hobbies? When were playing cards invented? Maybe they just sat and talked to each other. But Zee had no one to talk to. The air was silent. Even the birds who'd twittered in the morning darkness had flown off.

Finally she lay down on the couch in the atrium, pulling a lavender throw over her and wrapping her arms around herself, pretending they were David's arms and he was there with her. She had a whole silent conversation with him in her head. She began to feel much calmer, almost drowsy in the midday heat. Maybe nothing more would happen today, and there would be no reason not to have a swim. If David had left at three, surely he would be back soon. She stretched out, enjoying the feeling of being barefoot.

Then, with the loudest sound she'd ever heard, the earth seemed to split in two.

It took Zee a minute to realize it wasn't another earthquake. She ran to the bedroom and looked out. A column of dark gray smoke, thick and solid-looking, was rising from Vesuvius. She was fascinated in spite of her terror. The column rose and rose for the next few minutes. Within half an hour, it towered miles high, like the trunk of a giant tree. As the smoke at the bottom cleared, Zee saw that the entire top of the mountain, the snowy peak with its delicate point, was missing.

The gray column began to spread out, like an

umbrella with a flattened top. Nothing had reached her. The air was still clear, without traces of ash. She tried to remember what she'd read about Pompeii in school when she was a child. Maybe it was only the north section of the city that had been buried. She was, after all, almost at the southern gate. Maybe the south side escaped destruction.

But then came more explosions, one after another, and the umbrella spread farther and farther out. Ash began to fall, not gently like snow but as cinders flung with force. Rocks fell too, some the size of cats and dogs. It was three in the afternoon and as dark as night. She could see fires burning across the city.

When a chunk of pumice the size of a bed pillow crashed through the roof tiles and landed in the atrium, Zee grabbed her shoulder bag and David's knapsack and ran to the cellar room. She crouched in the cellar for what seemed to be hours, knees drawn up to her chin, her face buried in her arms. Shock wave after shock wave tore at the earth. The crocks of cheese and milk and oil tumbled from the shelves around her. In the first hour she'd lit one of the lamps, but the smoke, trapped in such a small room, made her feel like she was suffocating, and she extinguished it. The noise from the shock waves and the eruptions was deafening. Each time she heard the crash of falling debris, she imagined it piling up around the villa, slowly burying her alive.

It was too late. Even if David returned now, he could never free her.

She began to think about her life. How ironic it was that she'd fought to follow David to New Earth but was now going to die in a much older Earth, and much sooner than she'd imagined. She thought about how much she'd loved being an empath and how she felt she was starting to get the knack of divining using Major Dawson's new method. Like Major Dawson, she'd discovered that there was technology you could live without. She'd almost given up finding David when Arrius took her cube, but she'd found him anyway, just as Mrs. Hart had said, using her heart and her art. It was too bad she wasn't going to get to write that up for Major Dawson—he'd appreciate Ellie Hart's wit. She thought about little things, too. She'd take Pompeii's grilled fish over New Earth's nano hamburgers any day of the week, and hoped Marc was on his way to starting his own quiet food revolution. She hoped Melisande would become New Earth's most famous designer and Piper would have the baby she wanted.

Most of all, she hoped David would live. She hoped he would find someone who loved him as

much as she did, and someone he would love back. Tears slid from the corners of her eyes. She couldn't help it. With all her heart, she wanted him to be happy, but it hurt to want it. It hurt to leave.

The earth was rocking again. She felt she was being slammed back and forth between giant hands. The pig swung and slapped her in the face.

The rocking stopped, but the pounding noise continued. Something landed against the door with a thud. Probably a giant boulder.

"Zee! Zee, are you in there? Can you open the door?"

David!

Zee lunged to where she thought the door was but hit one of the shelves.

"Hang on," she said. "I'm looking for the door." She found it and yanked it open. The ambient glow of fire filtered through the cellar windows, lighting David's face. "How did you get to me?"

"I wrote down the coordinates of the cellar before I left."

She glanced down and saw Paul's body at David's feet. *He* was the boulder that had thudded against the door.

"Yeah," David said. "He put up a fight. I don't think Lorna's influence has quite worn off yet.

Fortunately, he had one of Mia's handy little stunners on him. I had to put him under. We have to get out of here fast, though. The air is getting worse, and I'm pretty sure we're trapped down here."

"How are we going to get back?" Zee asked. "We've only got two h-faxes and no computer capacity at all."

"Paul had an extra one with him. I thought he might. The man always overprepares. But the volcano is still playing havoc with the magnetic fields, and it took more energy than it should have to make it back, so the sooner we leave, the better."

David was already unfolding the three human faxes. The first and second began to hum and glow, even though their indicator numbers were dropping. The third one never revved.

Zee looked at David. "It's dead." David said nothing but immediately shut down the other two before more energy was wasted. "What are we going to do now? Is there anything you can do another energy transfer from?"

David shook his head. "Even if we had an energy source, we don't have that kind of time. So you're going to take Paul home. I'll stay here."

"I told you before. I'm not leaving without you." Zee took a deep breath. The air had begun to taste

faintly of ash. "Take Paul home, get Mia to do a remote transfer from the base. I can come back alone."

David considered for a minute, then shook his head. "Way too risky."

"I shouldn't have followed you here, and you shouldn't die because I did," Zee said firmly. "Only one of us needs to stay."

"Wait a minute," Paul said, coming to. "This was all my fault in the first place. If anybody has to stay, it's going to be me. Can somebody help me up? I feel a little out of it."

Startled, Zee and David both put out a hand and pulled him to his feet. His touch on Zee's palm was cool, without any of the fever she'd felt before.

"Hello, Paul," she said. "Welcome back."

"Lovely town you have here," he said. "But I outrank both of you, so if anyone has to stay, it will be me. And *none* of us is staying. Is that clear? We are three smart people, and we will get ourselves out of this. Agreed?"

"Agreed," David and Zee said.

"Then we'd better think fast."

After a moment of silence, Zee turned to David.

"Hold me." She put her arms around his neck and swung her feet off the ground.

"What are you doing, Zee?"

"I'm not that big, am I? Hold me, step onto the pad, and it will fax us both home. Even together I don't think we weigh more than some people."

David set her down. "Human faxing doesn't work by weight, Zee. It's about molecule count. The more molecules, the more energy it takes."

"Oh."

She looked down at her voluminous dress. All those little fibers woven together, all those particles. She wished she had some nano clothes. They were just one big molecule fused together.

But no one said they had to go back in any clothes at all.

"Wait a second," she said. "Maybe the volcano isn't eating as much energy as we think. Maybe it's also our clothes. The ones we got here. All those woven natural fibers. And our sandals and your knapsack. Why can't we just leave them here?"

David and Paul were looking at her like she was crazy. Then David jerked his tunic off over his head. "It's worth a try."

Zee rummaged in her shoulder bag until she found the clickstick with her computer on it. She took everything else off except the eagle talisman and left her clothes in a heap beside David's.

While Zee and David were stripping down, Paul

removed one of the power cells from his fax and clipped it into theirs. "Just a little booster," he said. "You've still got more molecules to transport than I do." Then he took off his clothes too.

David opened the faxes again. Zee put her arms around him and clung to him, the clickstick clutched in one hand. She hoped no part of her extended beyond the range of the fax beam. At the last minute, as the lights were beginning to strobe, she glanced back at her clothes and saw the little pouch attached to her discarded belt.

"Mrs. Hart's diamonds!"

"We don't need them, Zee," David said, holding her tight. "And they're a lot of molecules. Someone will find them someday."

"You're right. And even if they don't—" But she didn't finish because the flames of transmission began creeping up her legs.

The last things she felt were David's arms around her.

The last thing she heard was Mrs. Hart's voice in her head.

Now THAT was well done, Zee.

CHAPTER FOURTEEN

THE TRUTH OF CONSEQUENCES

Zee had to hand it to the Time Fleet Admiral. He never blinked an eye when three Fleeters without their clothes showed up in his transport room. He turned to Mia, who was standing beside him.

"Aariak, find them some clothes. Then all four of you report to my office. Clearly, we're in new territory here."

"Sorry about that," Mia said after he'd left the room. "He saw your incoming chip signals and got curious."

She left the room and came back in less than two minutes with T-shirts and drawstring khakis.

She'd even gotten socks and boots. For the first time in her life, Zee was glad to see her. Leaving their clothes behind had seemed natural in the race to escape, but now that they'd arrived, she felt very naked.

"How did you get these so fast?" Paul asked Mia, pulling on the tee. "I thought you'd be hung up in requisition for a good half hour. Rules and regulations, you know."

Mia snorted dismissively. "Who bothers with rules and regulations? Sometimes you just see a job and do it."

Zee felt better once she had clothes on.

"Let's go," David said. "Don't want to keep him waiting."

Zee hoped she'd have a chance to say good-bye to David before they sent her to the deportation unit. And she hoped she could make a convincing argument about why he shouldn't be punished as severely as she was. David, Mia, and Paul might get kicked out of the corps, but as a trainee she was sure she'd be sent to some punishment zone or other. Maybe back to Pompeii, just to make their point.

Admiral Walters's questioning began with Mia, who freely admitted she had transported both David and Zee without orders.

"It wasn't like that," Zee interjected. "I threatened her. She didn't have a choice."

Mia's head whipped around to look at her. "Do you *really* think I could be intimidated by you?" she asked. She turned back to the Admiral. "Really, sir, does that seem credible? At all?"

Zee tried to ease the way for David as well, pointing out that he had not wanted her to follow, she'd done it on her own initiative, and David had gone to unusually heroic lengths to save both Paul and her. It was impossible to tell from Walters's expression whether she'd made her case or not.

Zee had thought the questioning might go on for hours, but instead the Admiral said, "I know that each of you acted at some point to save the life of another. And even though you all went way out of bounds, you're all Time Fleeters. Which puts me in a difficult situation."

He opened a wall screen and went to a paragraph of text marked Section XXVI, Subsection xvi: Conduct and Goals. "Time Fleet Manual III-R, which I doubt any of you have ever read in its entirety. I draw your attention to point b of Subsection xvi: 'A Time Fleet member will obey any and all rules of conduct in the previous 2,045 pages, except when exercising judgment and discretion in aiding another Time Fleet member in peril.' "

He looked at them all soberly. "I'm older than all of you put together, and I've learned some things over the years. One of them is that there are times when the best thing to do is declare victory and go home. This is one of those times. So the official story will be that Paul Sutton encountered life-threatening difficulties on a solo field mission. David Sutton, aided and abetted by Mia Aariak, bypassed standard operating procedures to get aid to him as swiftly as possible. Zee McAdams remained behind, and when David Sutton did not return home from the Time Base Friday evening, alerted Time Fleet Central Command. A long-distance search and rescue was undertaken, and Time Fleet successfully transported both brothers home. Understood? Good. Sutton and Sutton will receive Hazardous Mission medals. Aariak will receive one for Humanitarian Service. McAdams will receive a written commendation for alerting Time Fleet Command. More than that I don't want to know. Dismissed."

Zee felt the deflation of relief mixed with dis-appointment. After everything they'd been through, to have her part in it officially erased seemed unfair.

David guessed how she was feeling and put an arm around her as they walked down the corridor. "Don't worry, Zee. There'll be other missions."

Paul glanced back and grinned at them. "Hey, you two, no physical contact on duty!"

"That's worth an official inquiry," Mia added.

"Who bothers with rules and regulations?" Zee responded, echoing Mia's earlier words back to her. "Sometimes you just see a job and do it."

A week later the dreaded summons came. Not from the Time Fleet but from David's parents. The Suttons were having another family dinner, and Zee would have given almost anything not to go. She was still getting over Pompeii—not the fear and destruction part of it, but the beautiful things she'd seen, how close she'd come to death, and how willing she and David had been to surrender their lives for each other. That meant more than anything else that had happened. More even than the night they'd spent together in the villa. She wondered where the family that lived there had ended up, and if Arrius had gotten away in time and whether anyone would ever find the diamonds or if they'd stay buried forever. She'd much rather have stayed home with David, who'd been there with her, than sit through an evening with future in-laws who didn't think much of her.

Zee would have liked to have gone straight from the base to the Suttons' house that night, but she knew that if she didn't dress up, David's mother would sneak frowning glances at her all evening. Remembering the colors of Pompeii, she found a dress at Meli's shop in vibrant saffron with long fitted sleeves that flared out just below the wrists and curved to a point at the bottom. The cuffs were lined with scarlet, Meli's spin on the medieval look. The dress made Zee feel like a princess. Or at least someone who could hold her own with David's parents.

At least she no longer had to worry about Paul. The effects of Lorna had worn off quickly and completely. Despite her computer's insistence that a human couldn't be literally infected by a silicon life-form, Zee had her doubts. She wanted to do more research on it when she had time. And she wanted to try her hand at nano design, to see if she could replicate some of the pieces of jewelry she'd seen in Pompeii. Just an item or two, when she had some free time.

Empathy and divining would always be Zee's true life's work. She had not forgotten the moments in Pompeii when she and her computer had seemed to discern each other's feelings. Restoring the computer had been one of the first things she did when she got back, and together they'd begun working on using the principles of empathy to facilitate communication between the two most intelligent life-forms on the planet, human and silicon.

The night was unseasonably warm, but Zee decided to wear the shawl Meli had insisted went with the dress. It was green with gold embroidery and matched her bracelet, the thin gold chain with the two Buddha charms, one jade and one gold, that David had given her long ago in the twenty-third century.

The front of the house was empty when they walked in. David looked confused.

"We didn't get the wrong night, did we?" Zee asked.

"They must be in the back."

David took her hand and led her through the dimly lit house. When they stepped into the garden, Zee saw a crowd of people. Lights came on and she saw bright lanterns woven through the trees. She saw David's sister standing beside the tiger, both wearing garlands of flowers. Then she saw Mrs. Sutton in a dress clearly inspired by the Roman empire.

"Quite the party your parents are throwing for you," she said to David.

"It's not for me, Zee," he whispered. "It's for you."

David let go of her hand and stepped away. Zee stood all alone. Everyone she knew on New Earth was there. Paul and Mia, Piper and her husband, Meli and the Lost Arts crowd. Marc presided over a long banquet table, and Major Dawson wore full dress uniform for the occasion. Mr. Sutton came up and handed her an empty glass.

While he poured champagne into it, he said in a low voice, "Paul told us the whole story, Zee. The *real* story about what happened in Pompeii." He turned to the crowd and held his own glass up. "To Zee. We are proud to welcome her to our family."

All the glasses went up. "To Zee."

"To Zee!"

⚝⚝⚝

Late that night, while David was sleeping, Zee slipped out of bed and went to her computer. She typed in the story of the evening—how wonderful it had been, how cold and crisp the champagne had tasted, and how Mia had given her her own personal human fax, saying, "Don't lose it. And don't tell Time Fleet Command you have it. It's still officially black ops."

Zee closed the file and put her fingers gently on the keyboard.

I have a question, she typed.

Yes?

Why did you help us in Pompeii? You risked your existence. I could have lost the clickstick, or not gotten out of Pompeii. So many computers want to destroy humans, yet you helped. Why?

Trust. And goodness. All intelligent life has the capacity for those two things, to the benefit of all. There is always goodness in the world.

Zee closed the screen gently and found her way back to bed. David turned, half waking, and stretched an arm out to her as she slipped into bed beside him.

"Everything okay?"

"Everything's wonderful."

She curled against him and felt the warmth of his body beside her and the weight of his arm over her. Goodness. There was always goodness in the world.